A TREASURY OF

African-American
Christmas Stories

VOLUME II

A TREASURY OF

African-American
Christmas Stories

VOLUME II

Compiled and edited by

Bettye Collier-Thomas

Henry Holt and Company
New York

Henry Holt and Company, LLC
Publishers since 1866
115 West 18th Street
New York, New York 10011

Henry Holt® is a registered trademark of
Henry Holt and Company, LLC.

Published in Canada by Fitzhenry & Whiteside Ltd.,
195 Allstate Parkway, Markham, Ontario L3R 4T8.

Library of Congress Cataloging-in-Publication Data
A treasury of African-American Christmas stories/
[compiled by] Bettye Collier-Thomas. — 1st ed.
p.   cm.
Vol. I: ISBN 0-8050-5122-8 (alk. paper)
Vol. II: ISBN 0-8050-6045-6
1. Christmas — Literary collections.   2. American literature —
Afro-American authors.   3. Afro-Americans — Literary collections.
I. Collier-Thomas, Bettye.
PS509.C56T73   1997   97-5459
810.8'0334-dc21   CIP

Henry Holt books are available for special promotions and
premiums. For details contact: Director, Special Markets.

First Edition 1999

Printed in the United States of America
1   3   5   7   9   10   8   6   4   2

We are grateful for permission to include the following previously copyrighted stories in this collection:

"Santa Claus Is a White Man" by John Henrik Clarke, published in *Opportunity,* December 1939. Reprinted by permission of the National Urban League.

"One Christmas Eve" by Langston Hughes. Copyright 1934 and renewed 1962 by Langston Hughes. Reprinted by permission of Alfred A. Knopf, Inc.

"A Carol of Color" by Mary Jenness, published in *Opportunity,* December 1927. Reprinted by permission of the National Urban League.

"A Christmas Journey" by Louis Lorenzo Redding, published in *Opportunity,* December 1925. Reprinted by permission of the National Urban League.

"It Came to Pass" by Bruce L. Reynolds, published in the *Chicago Defender,* December 23, 1939. Reprinted by permission of the *Chicago Daily Defender.*

To My Husband

Charles John Thomas

⊂⊃ CONTENTS ⊃⊂

⚝ ACKNOWLEDGMENTS ⚝

Compiling and editing this book forced me to take a closer look at the relationships among African-American culture, history, and fiction and to reexamine the meaning of Christmas. Through conversations with those who came to the many book signings for *A Treasury of African-American Christmas Stories,* my first book of Christmas stories (Henry Holt, 1997) as well as discussions with my students, colleagues, and other scholars, I have gained invaluable insights. James Turner, Alexa B. Henderson, Gloria Dickinson, Thelma Polk Collier, Sharon Harley, and Barbara Younger Catchings have encouraged my efforts and have given sage advice and counsel at every stage of this project. I owe a special debt of gratitude to V. P. Franklin, an exceptional friend, and one of the finest scholars I have ever known, for his meticulous reading of the manuscript. As always he raised critical questions and made insightful suggestions.

I consider myself to be one of the luckiest people in the world, to be so rich in friends and supporters. Over the years there are many people who have believed in me, advised me on all sorts of issues, supported me unconditionally, and provided intellectual sustenance. These include John Hope Franklin, Gerda Lerner, Nell Irvin Painter, C. Eric Lincoln, Richard C. Wade, Cheryl Townsend Gilkes, Samuel DuBois Cook, Mary Frances Berry, Genna Rae McNeil, H. Patrick Swygert, Timothy Jenkins, Lillian Williams, Rosalyn Terborg-Penn, Bettye J. Gardner, Sheila Gardner, Joyce Yette, Jing Lyman, Charles Ruff, Janet Sims-Wood, Thomas Battle, Giles Wright, and Clement Price.

Among the many people who responded positively to *A Treasury of African-American Christmas Stories* was Sandy Brewster Walker, the great-granddaughter of Augustus M. Hodges. Upon discovering that several pieces of Hodges's fiction were included in that book, she contacted me. I have learned a great deal about Hodges from the many conversations Sandy and I have had since then. She provided me with additional biographical information on Hodges and told me that his daughter Sarah was the model for "The Prodigal Daughter."

I would like to thank Mitsuru Sone Walker and Charles J. Thomas for typing the manuscript. Richard Woodland, Fatima Aliu, and Danielle Smallcomb provided research assistance in finding biographical data on the contributors and documentation for organizations and historical events referenced in some of the stories. Many other people, including Joanne Hawes Speakes and Marie McCain, contributed in various ways to making this project a success.

I also would like to thank Lee Daniels, director of Communications for the National Urban League, and Colonel Eugene Scott, general manager of the *Chicago Daily Defender*, for graciously responding to my requests for permission to reproduce several of the stories.

Charlotte Sheedy and Neeti Madan have shepherded all of my book-publishing projects and advised and encouraged me when I needed it most. Elise Proulx and Elizabeth Stein, my editors at Henry Holt, are among the most efficient editors I have known.

My husband, Charles J. Thomas, read each of the stories and made incisive suggestions for writing headnotes for several of them, including "Autobiography of a Dollar Bill," "General Washington's Christmas," "Fannie May's Christmas," "A Test of Manhood," and "Santa Claus Is a White Man." I am deeply grateful to him for his unstinting support of all of my work and for his devotion to me.

And, finally, I wish to thank my family, immediate and extended, for their unconditional support for all that I do. These include Katherine Bishop Collier, Joseph T. Collier, Jr., Thelma Polk Collier, Charles Gary Collier, Carlton Collier, Mildred Frazier, Ida Mae Thomas, Christine Lee, Frankie Oden, and Maurine Perkinson.

❧ NOTE TO READERS ❧

In order to maintain authenticity, as well as the flavor of the period, I have retained the original spelling, punctuation, paragraphing, and chapter and section divisions, except in cases of obvious typographical errors or where the meaning of the text was obscured. Nineteenth-century grammar, idioms, and punctuation deviate from those of today: writers sometimes used semicolons instead of commas, idiosyncratic capitalizations, and variations in spelling. In a few cases, letters have been added to complete the spelling of a word or a word has been inserted to ensure that a sentence is comprehensible. There are a few silent punctuation changes, but most alterations are indicated with brackets.

❧ INTRODUCTION ❧

Of all the holidays celebrated in America, Christmas is perhaps the most sacred and the most enduring among African-Americans. Its meaning is writ large in the struggle of black people for freedom and dignity. First celebrated by enslaved Africans, the holiday has evolved through generations who have embraced Christianity as a means of survival and have envisioned the birth of Christ as a new beginning. After the Civil War, the holiday became a time for reunion with family and friends and a time for reflection on the successes and failures of families, African-American communities, and the race. It was a time for renewing relationships and sharing family stories. It was a time for giving thanks to God for their very existence.

This collection of eighteen Christmas stories and two Christmas poems, originally published in black newspapers, periodicals, and journals between 1882 and 1939, is part of the rich African-American literary tradition that flourished after the Civil War. During the early 1970s I literally stumbled over these wonderful stories while researching my doctoral dissertation. The *Christian Recorder, Indianapolis Freeman, Baltimore Afro-American, Chicago Defender, Colored American Magazine, Opportunity,* and *Crisis* were among the foremost African-American publications at the turn of the century that published black writers. These publications were national in scope and were widely read throughout the United States. Were it not for the black newspaper and periodical press, few African-Americans would have been able to publish their writings.

This book represents only the second collection of African-American Christmas stories ever to be published. The first collection I compiled, *A Treasury of African-American Christmas Stories,* was published in 1997. That work included primarily writings from the late nineteenth century. The stories in this collection mostly appeared at later dates; twelve of the stories in this book were published in the period 1900 to 1939. At least one third of the writings are from the 1920s and are a part of the "New Negro" Movement, which found expression in what is popularly known as the Harlem Renaissance.

Black writers in the vanguard of this movement searched for a common ethnic identity and looked for heritage in folk and African culture. Their writing often reflected themes of cultural nationalism that emphasized that black people in the United States and throughout the world have a culture, style of life, worldview, and aesthetic values distinct from those of white Americans, white Europeans, and Westerners in general. Within this context Jesus Christ was defined and illustrated as being black, and literature, art, and music reflected a distinct African-American point of view. Writers such as Louis Redding, Georgia Douglas Johnson, Langston Hughes, John Henrik Clarke, and Mary Jenness spoke about American injustices and illustrated the gap between the promise of freedom and the reality of the African-American experience. Though today some of their writings may appear to be bitter and angry, placed in the context of their time, they are characteristically American. During the 1920s and 1930s, black writers, similar to their white counterparts, such as Sinclair Lewis, H. L. Mencken, and Ernest Hemingway, pointed to America's pressing social problems, and, like other writers, they used their art to address salient issues.

The 1997 publication of *A Treasury of African-American Christmas Stories* introduced the public to a literary tradition long forgotten. That collection of Christmas stories from a black perspective stimulated considerable comment, which suggested that the African-American tradition of writing Christmas stories was virtually unknown. Since few people had ever read a Christmas story written by, for, and about African-Americans, there was an assumption about what these stories should be. And because some of the themes involved controversial issues, a national discussion arose as to what constituted a "traditional" Christmas story. Some people were surprised to read Christmas stories that spoke of slavery, race relations, lynching, miscegenation, and other subjects that were predominant in United States history for over three hundred years. The sheer beauty of the stories and the compelling nature of the themes resurrected a tradition that had lain dormant for almost sixty years.

This second collection of Christmas stories extends our knowledge of the African-American literary tradition as it highlights the obscured writings of once well known black writers, journalists, and political activists, such as Pauline Hopkins, Augustus M. Hodges, Katherine Davis Tillman, Louis Redding, and John Henrik Clarke, as well as obscure figures like Lelia Plummer, J. B. Moore Bristor, J. B. Howard, Eva S. Purdy, and Bruce Reynolds. Because many of these authors now considered obscure were well known to the readers of black newspapers and periodicals, no biographical data were provided at the time these stories first appeared. As a result, very little is now known about some of the writers.

Although a number of these stories embrace controversial issues, most of the plots reinforce traditional values and themes that have defined the meaning of Christmas for centuries. The stories of Mary E. Lee, Mrs. J. B. Moore Bristor, and Bruce Reynolds stress that Christmas is about the birth of Jesus Christ and his gift to humanity. Mildred E. Lambert, Frederick Burch, Augustus M. Hodges, Margaret Black, and Louis Redding emphasize that Christmas is about loving, sharing, caring, and forgiving. Pauline Hopkins demonstrates the power of Jesus Christ to bring one to salvation and redemption. Lelia Plummer and J. B. Howard regard Christmas as a time for reflection on the past and accentuating one's heritage. Eva Purdy distinguishes the holiday as a time when all things are possible. Carrie Jane Thomas and Katherine Davis Tillman viewed Santa Claus as a force for good. In the 1930s, Langston Hughes and John Henrik Clarke, products of the Harlem Renaissance era, deconstruct traditional Christmas values and themes by stripping away the veneer of jolly old Santa Claus to expose the racist and anti-Christian views and practices that predominated in the white South at the time and that threatened the very existence of African-Americans. The Christmas poems written by Georgia Douglas Johnson and Mary Jenness reflect the "New Negro" ideology of the Harlem Renaissance era. Johnson compares the suffering of Christ with that of African-Americans and Jenness asserts that Jesus Christ was a black man.

This rich and complex collection of poems and stories reminds us once again of the enduring significance of the Christmas holiday among African-Americans. We are again allowed a glimpse into a past that highlights the love, hope, faith, aspirations, traditions, family values, spirituality, and fears common to our ancestors yesterday, and still meaningful to us today. These Christmas stories challenge us to see black men and women and their culture from the past in their terms and not our own.

A TREASURY OF

African-American
Christmas Stories

VOLUME II

Christmas Greetings

❧

GEORGIA DOUGLAS JOHNSON

Georgia Douglas Johnson

Georgia Douglas Johnson, born on September 10, 1877, in Atlanta, Georgia, was hailed as a significant literary figure by 1923. A graduate of the Atlanta University Normal School, in 1903 she married Henry Lincoln Johnson, a prominent attorney and Republican politician. In 1910, the family moved to Washington, D.C., where Henry established a law practice and in 1912 was appointed Recorder of Deeds for the District of Columbia by President William Howard Taft. Washington, D.C., with a highly educated and cosmopolitan African-American community and as the location of Howard University, was the catalyst that spurred Johnson to begin a literary career. She gained recognition in 1916 with the publication of three of her poems in *Crisis*, the magazine of the National Association for the Advancement of Colored People, and in 1918 with the publication of her first book of poetry, *The Heart of a Woman.* Initially criticized for her failure to explore racial themes, in 1922

Johnson published a book of poetry titled *Bronze: A Book of Verse* that addressed the issues of miscegenation and racism. In 1923 she wrote "Christmas Greetings" for the Christmas issue of *Opportunity,* the magazine of the National Urban League. In this poem, Johnson compares the suffering of Jesus Christ with that of African-Americans.

Christmas Greetings

Come, brothers, lift on high your voice,
The Christ is born, let us rejoice!
And for all mankind let us pray,
Forgetting wrongs upon this day.
He was despised, and so are we,
Like Him we go to Calvary;
He leads us by his bleeding hand,
Through ways we may not understand.
Come, brothers, lift on high your voice,
The Christ is born, let us rejoice!
Shall we not to the whole world say—
God bless you! It is Christmas Day!

A Carol of Color

❧

MARY JENNESS

Mary Jenness

In the original introduction to "A Carol of Color," Mary Jenness explained that the poem is written from the point of view of people of color, or "as the brown races see it." Pointing to the Christian tradition made familiar by the story of Ben Hur, she emphasized "that the three wise men came from Egypt, India, and Greece; thus typifying the worship of the Christ-child by the black, brown and white races." Published in *Opportunity* in 1927 during the Harlem Renaissance, "A Carol of Color" asserts that Jesus Christ was black or brown. It was during the time of the Harlem Renaissance that some African-Americans began to challenge the notion and image of a white Christ. Using biblical scripture that included, among other things, physical descriptions of Christ, the argument was made that Christ was black.

Although we know little about Mary Jenness, her "Carol of Color" reflects the "New Negro" ideology that emerged in the 1920s and explains black history, religion, and color in a positive vein.

A Carol of Color

∾

"I may not sleep in Bethlehem,
    Your inns would turn me back —
Because," said Balthazar, unsmiling,
    "My skin is black."

"I may not eat in Bethlehem,
    Your inns would frown me down,
Because," said Melchior, uncomplaining,
    "My skin is brown."

"Alone I ride to Bethlehem,
    Alone I there alight,
Because," cried Gaspar, all unheeding,
    "My skin is white."

Not one, nor two, but three they came,
    To kneel at Bethlehem,
And there a brown-faced Christ-child, laughing,
    Welcomed them.

The Autobiography of
a Dollar Bill

❧

LELIA PLUMMER

Lelia Plummer

"The Autobiography of a Dollar Bill" was published in the *Colored American Magazine* in December 1904. Little is known about Plummer since many of the early black newspapers and periodicals provided little or no biographical information on contributors.

"The Autobiography of a Dollar Bill" is a mixture of allegory and fantasy, describing the journey of "Mr. Dollar Bill." The story proposes a journey akin to the American slave experience, from the feelings of race memory, terror, landlessness, and claustrophobia during the Middle Passage to the severance of relations and relationships with the "ding, click" of the slave trade. Utilizing Christmas as a vehicle, and the dollar bill as a metaphor for the slave, Plummer examines the African experience in America. The dollar bill, like the slave, was a commodity that was constantly being traded, and both go through a succession of owners and have a myriad of experiences. Plummer explores the issues of bondage, status, self-definition, self-assertion, hope, and survival through "Mr. Dollar Bill" as he tells his story to a street-smart, homeless urchin named Jackie. As a benevolent owner, Jackie wants to keep his valuable possession, but circumstances dictate that this is impossible as he intends to treat himself to "pleasures" on Christmas Day. Thus, this valuable property must be passed on to a new owner in order for Jackie to improve his wretched condition.

Perhaps Plummer read and used as a model *The Interesting Narrative of the Life of Olaudah Equiano or Gustavus Vassa, the African, Written by Himself* (1789). In his revealing account of his experiences in slavery and freedom, Gustavus Vassa tells of his African heritage, being kidnapped, being sold to slave traders, his experience in the Middle Passage, the American plantation, and acculturation in America. Plummer's use of "Mr. Dollar Bill" in the role of a griot suggests how the oral tradition functioned to acculturate Africans to American slavery and to preserve African heritage among the enslaved. "Mr. Dollar Bill" tells of the experience of being surrounded by "heaps of others just like me"; being placed in a "great big, hollow, cold place"; being "snatched" and "plunged into darkness"; and conversing with elders who told him of their varied experiences in a bewildering world of uncertainty and confinement.

The Autobiography of a Dollar Bill

ॐ

It was Christmas Eve. The earth was covered with a white fluffy mantle. The snow gleamed brightly on the branches of the frozen trees, where a few brown little sparrows chirped cheerfully. The houses were covered with snow, and every few minutes might be heard the merry ringing of sleigh bells.

"Hullo" said ragged Jackie. "This is the kind of a Christmas for me, none o' yur mild dripping Christmases is this, but a good old-timer." The shivering little urchin addressed replied, that "As for them that has fires, a snowy Christmas [is] all right," but he was cold. "Anyway," he concluded, "it ain't Christmas, it's only Christmas Eve, and I want to know what you're going to do when Christmas really comes?"

"Well," said Jackie, "just now I'm goin' to sell my papers and earn some stray cash; then I'm goin' to that little corner of the bridge and cuddle down, and to-morrer, I'll treat myself with my cash." So away he trudged, crying "Paper here, sir, DAILY NEWS, and special Christmas numbers!" But few seemed to hear the little one, so intent were all upon their Christmas shopping. But suddenly in crossing the street, Jackie lost his footing and nearly fell under the heels of a dashing pair of horses, which were drawing an elegant equipage up the street. The coachman sprang down and kindly raised the little arab in his arms. "Why youngster, you want to be careful! Are you hurt?" Then the carriage door opened and a kind face looked out upon little Jackie, who was endeavoring to wrest himself from the coachman's arms.

"Are you hurt, little fellow?" a sweet voice asked. "No um" responded the blushing Jackie. Then seeing his rags, a kind hand drew forth some money from a bag and slipped it into the newsboy's hand. The coachman took his seat, and in a moment the carriage had passed on.

Jackie gazed upon the money in his dirty little hand, scarcely able to believe his own eyes. Yes, in that brown little palm lay a clear, crisp one dollar bill. Jackie hugged himself with delight, and clasping his dollar closely, danced off to resume his efforts to sell his papers. But people did not bother with Jackie any more that day, and when night came he had not sold one paper. Nevertheless his heart felt very light and he was happy. Many, many times during the day he had stolen a glance at the crisp little bill; and now when the bright and beautiful lights began to appear in the city street, he rushed off to his little niche in the bridge where he was pleased to curl himself up for the night. "This here's better'n them old homes where you'r all tucked and cuddled like a girl" he used to say to his young companions. There he cuddled down, still hugging closely his precious dollar bill and thinking of the pleasures it would bring him Christmas day. Suddenly, to his surprise, he heard a squeaking little voice call "Jackie, say Jackie!" Jackie rubbed his eyes and looked around. He saw no one. Suddenly it came again, and this time Jackie did not look for it, but said, "All right, here I am; what do you want anyway?"

"See here, Jackie," the voice continued, "I'm Mr. Dollar Bill and I want to tell you all about me. But hug me up nice and tight, for night is cold." Jackie tightened his clutch upon the precious bill. "Now, I first sprang into this world of wonderful things in a place where I saw heaps of others just like me. Oh my, there were so many of them that my eyes just ached! And there were round little men who were very bright looking but kept very humble before me, for they seemed to know that they were not half so good or valuable as I.

"Then there were some little silvery things, whom we called, 'little dimes,' and I believe there were more of them than any of us could ever imagine. Well, I stayed in this a good while, until I got really tired; at last somebody far larger and better clothed than you, Jackie, took me and put me in a great big, hollow, cold place. If I had been alone I would not have liked it at all, but there were lots of others just like me, only none of the shining things were there. I asked some of the more important men what it meant and they said 'Little ones were to be seen and not heard' and that I must live and learn. But I was not there long, for a great broad hand came and hauled me out. I felt myself being whirled through the air for a few moments, then I was suddenly plunged into utter darkness. Ah Jackie! that was a black moment for me. I could not tell where I was. For a long while I felt as if I were moving. Then suddenly, I was whisked out again and put into a little, wee box and felt myself scudding along at a terrific rate. I wondered where I was going. I was snatched from there just as suddenly, but before I was again plunged into darkness, I caught a gleam of bright and pretty things and a great moving mass of people. Jackie, where was I?"

"Oh I guess somebody went to do some Christmas shopping as they call it, with you and took you into one of those beautiful stores."

"Very good" replied the bill complacently. "You're not a bad little chap for your age, Jackie, not at all. Well, to proceed with my tale, I met there an old friend, Jackie. Yes, my boy, an old friend, for I myself have had so many travels that I am beginning to feel old, though I look so bright and new. The last time I had seen him was when we lay in a great box together. He recognized me instantly and I began to talk to him. 'Hullo, old fellow!' I said, 'Here we are again. Now where have you been?' Then I noticed that beside him lay a very old and tattered gentleman, at whom I was inclined to turn up my nose, but bless me, Jackie, my friend seemed more inclined to notice the old one than he did me, the bright, the new and pretty. Just then came a ring and a click and my friend was gone.

"Then the old tattered fellow looked at me seriously and soberly for a few minutes, and began, 'An old fellow like myself, youngster, is really more valuable than a young one, like you. Oh! young ignorance, if you only knew the many and varied tales I could tell! Ha ha! youngster, you look as if you thought you knew something.' Then I [blushed] and looked down, for do you know, Jackie, I didn't just like the way the fellow was talking. But he kept on. 'Why, green one, I have travelled across rough waters, over green fields. I have been in the home of the rich, where there were many, many more like myself, and I have been in the homes of the poor, where there were none like myself. Little one, I have been where all was innocence and purity, and likewise where all was crime. Yes I have been snatched from wallets by crime-stained hands and been in the pockets of noted criminals. What phase of life have I not seen? I have been the poor man's joy, the miser's hoard, and until I fall in pieces, I shall continue to travel these rounds.' Ding, click! My acquaintance was gone.

"There were lots of other bills there, who, I do not doubt, were worthy of my notice, but really, Jackie, that last wonderful fellow had scarcely gone, when rude hands snatched me, sped me through space, and once more consigned me to gloom. But I did not mind the darkness so much this time, for I reflected upon the old one's story and hoped that I might live to be the ragged, worn old fellow he was. You see so much more of life, Jackie. While I studied and thought, I could hear sweet voices speaking and suddenly a kindlier and gentler hand gave me into your keeping. Some way or other I took a fancy to you directly. You seemed to treat a fellow as if he had some feeling and you had some consideration for it. I really like you, Jackie, and when Christmas morning comes and I am leaving you, for I suppose I must, do not grieve for I shall always be on the watch for you again."

"Oh no, You shall never go," cried Jackie with energy. He gave a start and sprang to his feet. It was early, early in the blessed Christmas morning and already the bells were chiming the birth of the Babe at Bethlehem. How they rang in Jackie's ears and heart.

"What! have I been dreaming all this? Not a bit of it! I heard that dollar just as plain as I hear these bells and I know that even if I part with my dear old bill, he'll be on the lookout for me and some day I'll have him again."

Mollie's Best Christmas Gift

❧

MARY E. LEE

Mary E. Lee

Mary E. Ashe Lee, the daughter of Simon S. and Adelia M. Ashe, was born free in Mobile, Alabama, on January 12, 1851. In 1860 her family moved to Xenia, Ohio, the site of Wilberforce University, one of the first institutions of higher learning to be established for African-Americans in the United States. Founded by the African Methodist Episcopal Church (AME), the school included what was known as a "normal" department that provided primary and secondary instruction for black children and adults in addition to the college course. Mary enrolled in the college course and graduated with a B.S. degree in science from Wilberforce in 1873. As a student, she distinguished herself as a poet and essayist, and following graduation she taught in the public schools of Galveston, Texas. In December 1873 she married Benjamin Franklin Lee, who enjoyed a noted career as Professor of Theology and President of Wilberforce University. In 1892 he was elected a bishop of the AME Church.

During the late nineteenth century Mary E. Lee was well known as a poet, fiction writer, and religious worker in the AME Church. Her articles, poems, and short stories appeared in the *Christian Recorder, AME Quarterly Review, Ringwood's Journal,* and other publications. During the 1890s the Lee family resided in Philadelphia, where Mary was affiliated with the Women's Christian Temperance Union, the Ladies' Christian Union Association, and the AME Women's Mite Missionary Society. In 1892 she was elected vice-president of the Afro-American Press Association.

"Mollie's Best Christmas Gift" was published in the *Christian Recorder* in December 1885. Lee wrote the story to emphasize the importance of putting Christ back in Christmas. The Christmas celebration, introduced in the United States during the late eighteenth century, was, by 1865, officially recognized by most states as a legal holiday. By 1850 the celebration had taken on its more modern character, with feasting and gift-giving being the foremost focus. Lee's concern in 1885, the year this story was written, is echoed today by many people, especially parents who are besieged by children who view Christmas simply as a time to receive toys and presents.

"Mollie's Best Christmas Gift" not only imparts a message for Christians, but it provides the reader with a glimpse of what

Christmas was like for middle-class African-American children in the late nineteenth century.

Raised as a free black child of privilege, Mary Lee spoke from experience. Little is known about the reading and recreational habits of black children in that period but, in this story, we learn that they read history books, such as *Pilgrim's Progress* and *Line upon Line*, and fairy tales like "Cinderella," "Puss in Boots," and "Beauty and the Beast."

Lee's message in "Mollie's Best Christmas Gift" is simple yet profound. It is that Christmas is about the birth of the Christ child, and that the best present a child can receive is the Bible, which provides one the opportunity to know and to understand the teachings of Jesus.

Mollie's Best Christmas Gift

ର

Mollie's parents had been "well-to-do," and she had always looked forward to Christmas as a day of joy and merriment. She awoke Christmas morning to find her stockings filled or the Christmas tree laden with toys and good things. Among her presents were so many fairy stories, including of course, "Cinderella," "Puss in Boots," "Beauty and the Beast," etc. So, she also had "Line upon Line" and "Pilgrim's Progress." A week before the Christmas in which our story begins, Mollie had been trying to decide in her mind what she would like to get on Christmas as a present. She had almost every kind of toy, so she could think of nothing new that she had not had on previous holidays. She consoled herself with the hope that her parents and friends would think of something new and beautiful. But the circumstances of her parents had changed; her father found himself less able than he had ever been before to provide many presents for the children so he concluded to buy only such things as would be useful.

Mollie, herself, was somewhat changed from what she had been on other Christmases. She was older now and more thoughtful. She had a restlessness [which she did not understand], a feeling that there was some duty she had neglected, with an undefined desire for something which she might have attained, but had not. Thus she looked forward to Christmas. What was her chagrin when she found that her presents consisted of only a pair of shoes, a dress and a silver dollar! She was so greatly disappointed in receiving what she considered no present — only the things necessary to her comfort, which her father would provide for her at any time — that she hid her face in the folds of her blue merino dress to conceal her tears; then looking around she saw under the mantle a parcel addressed thus: "To Mollie from her brother, Joseph." It contained a book, "The Prince of the House of David." She began that day to read her book and carefully read it with growing interest in the history day by day. Of course she had long since learned the story of the cross, both at home and at the Sunday school, though she had not felt that she had a personal concern in it. But in reading this book, Jesus of Nazareth appeared to her the fairest among ten thousand and altogether lovely. Yet she thought the book might not be true. Perhaps these letters were not written by the Alexandrian maiden, after all. But, she [told herself], "The Bible tells the story. I will read my Testament." So she began to read the story of Jesus in her Testament as she had never read it before. There was new light upon the pages as she read; light grew lighter and lighter until her heart seemed to run over with love and sympathy for Christ and to melt with shame at her own unworthiness.

It was New Year's morning; for one week she had been reading and thinking of Jesus, and her Christmas gifts resulted in the happiest New Year she can ever have on earth, for then she first received Jesus, the hope of earth and joy of heaven, as her Saviour. Ever since then she has felt like saying to little girls and boys just giving up their childish toys, "Remember now thy Creator in the days of thy youth."

A Christmas Story

೮

CARRIE JANE THOMAS

Carrie Jane Thomas

"A Christmas Story," published in the *Christian Recorder* in 1885, is a traditional children's fable with mystical characters and magical events, including the mythical Santa Claus. It is a moral parable whose message to children is, "be good and obedient to your parents and believe in Santa Claus and all your wishes will be granted."

The story focuses on Minnie Leslie, a ten-year-old girl, one of four children who lives with her parents in comfortable middle-class surroundings. The Leslie children have been encouraged to believe in Santa Clause and warned that if they are disobedient he will not leave them toys and gifts. Minnie, influenced by Lucy, a girlfriend, determines to stay awake to see Santa Claus and to dispute the claims of Lucy, who argued that Santa Claus was none other than Minnie's parents.

Although little is known about Carrie Jane Thomas, she obviously was very interested in writing children's literature. "A

Christmas Story" was written for middle-class black children, whose expectations of Santa Claus and Christmas paralleled those of their white counterparts. Unlike the Santa Claus depicted fifty years later by Langston Hughes in "One Christmas Eve" and John Henrik Clarke in "Santa Claus Is a White Man," Thomas's traditional Santa Claus is universal in his love for all children. He could, and did, serve the purpose of middle-class parents who used him as a kind of surrogate parent to maintain discipline and instill important values in their children.

A Christmas Story

৽

It is Christmas night and Mr. and Mrs. Leslie are seated in their cozy parlor surrounded by their four children, Kittie, Susie, Willie, and Minnie, who is papa's pet and allowed to do almost as she pleases. They are talking about the one thing Christmas brings—Santa Claus—each busy telling what is wanted. They keep such chattering you can scarcely hear your ears. When Mr. Leslie says, "children, it is ten o'clock," all the noise is stopped at once and their faces become very sad, for they all know that it is their bedtime, and, knowing their father's rules, not one dares protest, although the time has passed unusually quick. At last the silence is broken by "Pet" [Minnie].

"I am not going to bed at all tonight, papa; I am determined to see Santa Claus this night, for Lucy Bennett told me, when we were coming from school, that ma and pa were the Santa Claus and they put all the things into our stockings; but I told her I did not believe it. I am ten years old and never saw Santa Claus in my whole life, so I shall sit up all night."

"Well, you won't get anything," says Kittie.

"I don't care for anything, but to see Santa Claus," [answers Minnie].

Her mama smiled and said, "I am afraid my little girl could not bear the sight of Santa, even if she could stay awake until he comes, which is very doubtful."

"I know he won't give you anything, 'cause you is so 'quisitive," says Willie. "All the reason you gets anything is because he feels sorry for a poor tongue-tied boy like you that can't talk plain," [responds Minnie].

"You won't be so fierce in the morning, when you begin to beg," retorts Willie.

"Willie!" calls his mother, "you ought to be ashamed of yourself to tease your sister so; go to bed this moment."

All of the children trooped off to bed. Momma and papa went up to their room, leaving poor Minnie all alone. "As the stockings were all hung in the parlor," Minnie says to herself, "he is obliged to pass through here and I will sit close to my own stocking so I can see when he goes to put the goodies in." Minnie exclaims, as she hears the clock strike eleven, "I am so glad it is eleven, I won't have to wait long. They say he always comes at twelve." If poor Minnie had known what she was destined to see at twelve, she would have gone to bed. But she did not, and so the time goes by and it is almost twelve o'clock. Minnie is so sleepy. She looks at the clock, only a quarter to twelve. "I cannot go to sleep. I must see him, and, besides, how they will laugh when I tell them I got sleepy and could not wait." Just then she goes off, and the clock strikes twelve. The door opens and in walks Santa Claus, followed by twenty of his confederates. Santa Claus himself is a little fat man with white, bushy beard and white hair covered with a frost of many winters. He has a doll for Kittie, a horse and wagon for [Willie], dresses for Sue, and, in fact, everything they all wanted, but for Minnie he had nothing. Minnie began to whimper.

"What is the matter?" asks Santa, in a gruff voice, as if he had just seen her.

"I want something, too."

"There will be more than you want presently," and he proceeded to fill the stockings. When he had filled all but Minnie's, he gave a whistle and marched through the room and passed out, followed by another whom she had not seen. His name was on his cap and Minnie saw that it was Disobedience. He was loaded with articles of every description. Minnie saw her blue silk dress, which she remembered wearing to an evening party when her mother told her not to do so. Then there was her last birthday present, a silver cup from papa, which her mother told her never to carry to the spring, but she disobeyed and dropped it into the spring. There were many other things, too numerous to mention. All this Minnie took in at a glance. He passed on and another took his place; he had scraps of rick-rack, crochet and knitting dangling from head to foot; he also carried a box in his hand which was filled with dolls' clothes, dresses and aprons without sleeves and without hems; there were the mittens she promised to Widow James, but never finished. He passed on and another came in with Minnie's books, torn and scratched, with dolls' heads, and crippled men and women drawn on them, which would make you laugh to see. The next had half worn shoes and stockings, which might have been given to some poor children, but Minnie had allowed them to lie around out of doors until they were unfit for use. Another came in making such horrible faces that Minnie covers her face with her hands and begins to scream, which awakens her to find that she has only been dreaming. She is as cold as she can be, for the fire has gone out and the room is dark. Minnie jumps up and goes to bed, where Kittie has been for at least three hours. Next morning the children were up searching their stockings, which were filled with everything they had asked for, and to Willie's surprise, Minnie's stocking was overflowing. You may be sure that was a memorable Christmas [for] Minnie, and I need not tell you that she is over forty years old and she has never tried waiting for Santa Claus again.

Fannie May's Christmas

⧫

KATHERINE DAVIS TILLMAN

Katherine Davis Tillman

Katherine Davis Chapman Tillman was born in Mound City, Illinois, on February 19, 1870, and at an early age evidenced a special talent for writing. Encouraged by her mother, a gifted teacher and writer, she soon gained a reputation as a poet. In 1888 the *Christian Recorder* published "Memory," her first poem. Her first short story appeared in *Our Women and Children* magazine, published by the American Baptist Publication Society. She soon became famous for her poetry and prose, which appeared in all of the leading African-American newspapers and periodicals.

A graduate of Yankton High School in South Dakota, she also attended the State University at Louisville, Kentucky, and Wilberforce University. Around 1890 she married George M. Tillman, an African Methodist Episcopal (AME) minister. As a Christian feminist activist, Tillman became editor of the *Women's Missionary Recorder*, and served as secretary of the Iowa Branch of the Women's Mite Missionary Society for twelve years and as president of the North Missouri Conference Branch. Like many female church leaders, she was active in the black women's club movement. She was honorary president of the City Federation of Colorado Springs and honorary president of the California Federation. She was director of the Baby Department of the National Association for Colored Women's Public Posters and Prints, where she monitored the publication and distribution of posters and prints illustrating negative images, frequently derogatory caricatures of African-American children. In 1919 she targeted the Gold Dust Twins, a popular and highly success-ful caricature of black children who were depicted in a variety of comical and demeaning antics on posters, playing cards, and other materials. She organized clubs throughout the United States to protest the N. K. Fairbank Company, the distributors of the materials. Although Tillman did not succeed in having the material removed from the market, the firm toned down the images.

Tillman was an ardent feminist, and in an 1893 *AME Church Review* article entitled "Some Girls That I Know" she stated, "There is one phase of my literary career that I thoroughly enjoy, and that is the privilege of writing to the young women of my race. Sometimes I address myself to them in stories, as in 'Our Ruth,' sometimes in poetry, but always I have an earnest desire to reach them and help them." And so in 1921 she wrote "Fannie May's Christmas," which was published in the *Christian Recorder*. The subtheme of this short story is gender issues.

The setting of "Fannie May's Christmas" is Christmas 1877, in Louisville, Kentucky. Fannie May is an eight-year-old only child in a poor but hard-working family, who has been informed that Santa probably will not visit her for Christmas because times are too hard and her mother is ill.

Under these dire circumstances, Fannie May and her family, together with friends and church members, work hard to make gifts and prepare goodies to share at Christmas. Through these efforts and another blessed event, the true meaning of Christmas is discovered and celebrated by Fannie May and her community.

Fannie May's Christmas

ॐ

It was a long time ago, for it was in 1877 that Fannie May, a dear little girl with brown face and long, silky braids of hair, of which she was very proud when it was properly beribboned, lived on York Street in the city of Louisville [Kentucky]. In addition to her beautiful hair, Fannie May had other attractions. She had bright, black eyes that seemed ever to hold a smile lurking in their depths and a disposition that made her loved from one end of the street in which she lived to the other.

Fannie May's father worked across the street, in the big tobacco factory on the corner where he and a hundred others of Negro-American ancestry stemmed and packed tobacco for shipping.

Fannie May's mother, a fair little woman of frail physique, worked for a kind white family when she was able. Living was very high in this beautiful Southern city, and when May's father had paid the exorbitant rent demanded by his white landlord for their two-room home, kept fire in the kitchen stove, and in the grate fire place in the living room, brought wood and the cheapest kind of clothing, there was very little left of the seven dollars and a half pay that he received each week. Then, too, as her father would have told you himself, he was a typical Kentuckian of that day, and a laboring man must have his morning toddy, and the little store on the corner with its bar in the rear sometimes got a third of his week's pay.

So you see when Fannie May's mother was ailing as she had been now for several weeks and could not go to work for her "white folks," it looked mighty, mighty, slim for Christmas doings at Fannie May's humble little home.

And since there were just two things, out of all the things in the whole round world, that Fannie May had set her heart on, it did seem as if a little girl who didn't act greedy and ask for lots and lots of things like May Bell and Prudie Ann, two of her little friends, might have those two things.

But while Fannie May was only eight, she had lots of sense, and Grannie Hope, who lived next door, always declared she was "old in the head," because she was so thoughtful.

She spoke of these two things as she ate her share of corncake and sorghum at supper.

"I just wish Santy Claus would bring me just two things out of all the millions of things he's got in his sleigh," she sighed.

"What's that, Fannie May?" said her father, who was very fond of his little daughter.

"I wants a great big doll, that can shut its eyes and go to sleep when

I rock it and say 'mamma' when you squeeze it; and then I wants a great big cradle bed, to put it to sleep in. Me and Prudie Ann and May Bell saw one [in] the store when we took the white folk's clothes home. Oh, pappy, it was just beautiful. If I had a big doll and bed, I wouldn't want another thing. All the other children get something to play with but me. I ain't got no little brother and sister, nor nothing 'tall."

Fannie May's father's face grew long. "Don't look for nothing this Christmas, cause I done heard tell Santa Claus wouldn't be able to get around to our place at all, cause times is so hard."

Fannie May's bright eyes filled with tears. "An I ain't going to get nothin 'tall," she said. "How come he ain't coming here this Christmas. He never missed before?"

"Times too hard and mamma's sick."

"I would got something off the Sunday-school Christmas tree, but I done missed fo' Sundays staying with mamma, and when you done missed fo' Sundays, Prudie Ann and May Bell both say you don't get nothin' off the Christmas tree," and overwhelmed by the tragic turn of affairs Fannie May wept aloud.

Fannie May's mother, who was in bed, roused right up. She always did, if there was anything the matter with Fannie May. Mothers are like that, you know.

"Stop crying! mother's child," she said. "Indeed, you will have something for Christmas, soon as I feel the least bit better; I'll begin right away making some new Christmas clothes for Ella Virginia."

Fannie May's most cherished possession was a big rag doll, made by her mother out of flour sacking and stuffed with bran from a neighboring lumber yard. Her face was outlined with bluing and on her head was real hair, cut from Fannie May's mother's head. Ella Virginia had been Fannie May's pride since she was five. She shared all of her games of play-house and was hugged close to her bosom when Fannie May went to sleep, but constant wear with an active little mistress like Fannie May had reduced Ella Virginia to a mere wreck of her former self. She had leaky arms and legs. Her face was so soiled that it was hard to discover where [her] eyes had been, and even Fannie May's loving heart ached at the sorry appearance of Ella Virginia beside the china dolls owned by Prudie Ann and May Bell.

The last time the trio had a sewing bee for their doll children, over in Prudie Ann's back yard, Fannie May's friends had so openly poked fun at Ella Virginia that the little mother had arisen in righteous wrath and hied herself homeward—her eyes filled with angry tears—but the sad fact remained unchanged—Ella Virginia's best days were past. She could still be loved and played with alone at home—but out, never! Still it would not be fair to Ella Virginia to refuse new clothes for her. Her mother could make such a cunning little jacket and such pretty dresses for Ella Virginia, and she worked real button holes in her clothes, and Fannie May could button them just as she did her own clothing.

She assented tearfully and went about her dishes as cheerfully as she could, but her little heart was sad, oh so sad, because she of all the little girls in her street would have no visit from Santa Claus at Sunday school or at home.

When Fannie May's last dish was washed and placed upon the cupboard shelves and she had read a chapter in the New Testament, with her father, she sat in her own little red rocker that her father's kind dark hands had made for her on her last birthday, and looked in the big fire place and imagined how wonderful it would be if on Christmas Eve she could hang her stocking up, just as she did last Christmas, and wake up and find it all crammed to the toe with good things—candy and nuts and a big yellow orange from far-away Florida or California, and a big doll and a sure-enough cradle-bed, big enough to put her to sleep in, and—but the little eyes had closed, for the Sandman had managed to throw a good, big handful of sand in them, I suppose, and Fannie May tumbled out of the little red rocker to the floor and her father picked her up and kissed her and put her to bed.

When he was through, Fannie May's mother was crying, for she had been watching Fannie May, and she knew what she was thinking about, for she knew what she thought about at Christmas time when she was like Fannie May and she knew that it breaks a child's heart when she is told to expect nothing for Christmas.

"Billie Boy, Fannie May's so little. She don't know anything about hard times. She must have a Christmas. Oh, and here I am sick and can't get out to work."

"Why, look here! It isn't fair for a poor man like me to have two babies on his hands at once," [said Fannie's father,] with an awkward pat on his sick wife's head. "But don't worry, she shall have some Christmas if I have to set up every night for a month. I'm going to make her a doll cradle-bed, big enough for a sure-enough baby, just as she is fretting about. I've got some nice pine that will be just the thing and you can make the mattress between grunts," he added with a mischievous smile.

Fannie May's mother was young, so she clapped her thin brown hands together almost as Fannie May would have done. "And, Billie Boy, I can make the little sheets and pillow cases and tack a comfort. I'm so glad you thought of such a beautiful thing to do. I know it will be just fine, because you made Fannie May's little rocker so nice."

"Then, too," said Fannie May's father, his face all smiles, "you know Granny Hope's a powerful hand for molasses cookies and molasses candy, and we've got plenty of sorghum laid by, and if I can get hold of a few walnuts for the candy, I guess Fannie May'll feel pretty good after all, except for the doll and I don't see how we can manage that unless one drops down from the skies somewhere."

"Like the Babe of Bethlehem," sighed the mother. "Well, I'll do all I can to make Ella Virginia presentable."

Night after night found Fannie May's father sitting up after a hard day's work at the factory, working on the cradle-bed. Sometimes he would fall asleep at his task, but when he did, he always got up an hour earlier in the morning and made up for it. He had to hide it at Granny Hope's, next door, to keep Fannie May from knowing. At last it was finished, and when he brought it home after Fannie May was asleep, Fannie May's mother was too happy for anything. "Oh, how could you make such a beautiful, beautiful bed, all by yourself?" she said.

For the cradle bed was wonderfully carved with the figure of an angel at the head, and it had nice even slats and rockers just like a true bed.

"It is big enough for a real baby, sure enough," said the mother.

Then they began to plan again about the cookies and candy. Yes, Granny Hope would make them. Fannie May's mother had done her more than one good turn when she was down with her back, and they needn't bother one mite about the walnuts, for she had some nice, fresh ones her son had sent in from the country, and she would make walnut taffy like she used to make at the "Big Houses" at Christmas times, before the War. Of course she meant the Civil War that freed the American slaves.

Fannie May knew nothing of these delightful doings, but she was more cheerful than she had been for she was busy making presents for others. Out of an old red flannel shirt Granny Hope gave her, she made a needle case for her mother and stitched the edges with coarse black thread and a penwiper for her father; then she made two iron holders for Granny and covered them with some scraps of ticking, and for Prudie Ann and May Bell she made the dearest little pin cushions. Did you know there was so much Christmas in a discarded red flannel shirt? Of course there was magic in Fannie May's little fingers, the magic of love, and we can all have that if we work hard enough for it.

You remember I told you that everybody liked Fannie May because of her pleasant disposition. Well, Prudie Ann and May Bell and the day school teacher and the Sunday school teacher all missed the bright eyed little one with the sunny smile, and when the children told the teachers how Fannie May's mother was sick, and Santa Claus wouldn't be able to bring Fannie May not a speck of Christmas, both of the teachers felt so sorry and said to themselves that something must really be done about it, for it really wasn't right for a little girl who minded her parents and teachers and did her work well at home and school and seldom ever pouted, should have to go without Christmas. The day teacher, a young woman who had struggled very hard to get through school herself, went to work that very day and began to crochet Fannie May the dearest little blue hood, just like all the fortunate little girls were wearing that winter and then she ripped up a blue skirt that she had outgrown, cleaned and pressed it and made Fannie May a little blue cape to match the hood and bought and sewed three shiny gold buttons down the front. The Sunday-school teacher, who was a very busy woman with a big family of her own, took time and went to see Fannie May's mother, to learn just exactly what Santa Claus might be expected to do for Fannie May at Christmas. They had a nice visit, then the teacher saw the superintendent and gave him the size of the little girl's shoes, and he said the Sunday-school Santa Claus would be happy to put a nice new pair of shoes on for Fannie May, together with the regular treat, and the teacher thanked him and bought a pair of stockings to go with the shoes, and they [hung] them on the Christmas tree with two hundred pink, red, yellow, white and blue bags of candy and nuts.

Christmas Eve night, the day teacher, who had the [hood] and cape all done [and] tied up in nice, smelly paper, with a blue ribbon, came by for Fannie May to go to the Christmas tree. It was the first time she knew she was going to get to go.

"Oh! Oh!" she fairly screamed. "Going to the Christmas Tree! Going to the Christmas Tree! Got a new blue hood; got a new blue cape." She danced up and down with joy.

Her mother and day teacher were happy too. By and by, here came Prudie Ann and May Bell to see if Fannie May could go, and Oh, she could, and her silky braids looked so pretty under the new hood, and the cape was just right, and Oh, wasn't it just a beautiful world after all—a beautiful Christmas world!

At the church a wonderful Christmas tree sparkled with candles and gifts, and the superintendent told of the Babe of Bethlehem, in whose honor the gifts were made. There was a concert, two dialogues, songs and speeches about Christmas. The day teacher held the children spellbound with "The Night Before Christmas," and at the close, the gifts were distributed. Fannie May got a pair of shoes, stockings, a pink bag of candy, and a little china doll, jointly contributed by her two little friends. How happy she was when she took her things home, but when she rushed up to the door, she found that mamma was not well enough to be disturbed, and that she was to sleep next door at Granny Hope's and her father added that Granny said she had better hang up her stocking for she had heard that Santa Claus might come by after all.

Fannie May didn't really mind staying with Granny, but she would rather have stayed home on this particular night to talk over all that had taken place. Over at Granny Hope's she snuggled under the warm Irish chain quilt and peeped out every little while to see if she could see any sign of Santa Claus, but alas, the Sandman got her and it was bright day when she heard Granny stirring, and jumping out of bed cried quickly, "Christmas Gift! Granny, Christmas Gift!"

"Oh, you caught me, did you, you little Booger," said Granny, and gave her a big red apple and then Fannie May rushed to the fireplace, for there was the stocking she had hung up the night before, fat and mysterious looking. In it she found molasses cookies, candy and a ginger-bread man.

Fannie May rushed into her clothes and hurried over home.

But what was that standing in the middle of the kitchen floor? A cradle-bed! The prettiest you ever saw, big enough for Ella Virginia, or a live baby, and it had a mattress and pillows and the daintiest comforter imaginable.

"Oh, papa! Oh, mamma!" she cried, rushing into the other room, but she stopped still for her mother was taking medicine from a glass her father held and Granny, who had come in another way was holding something up in her arms—something that looked like a doll— something tiny and brown and wrinkled, but Oh, so very dear—something that you loved the very minute you laid eyes on it, and wanted to hold it in your arms.

"Oh, mamma, it isn't a live baby, is it?" cried the happy child, as Granny laid it in her arms for a wee moment.

"Yes, it is your Christmas Gift—your own, dear, little baby brother! Will you let him lie in your cradle-bed when he is sleepy?"

"Oh, mammy! Oh, daddy!" cried Fannie May; "I thought I wasn't going to have any Christmas at all, and it's the best Christmas in the whole world, isn't it? Didn't God give us a good Christmas this time?"

A Christmas Sketch

❦

MILDRED E. LAMBERT

Mildred E. Lambert

Mildred E. Lambert, described by the *Christian Recorder* as "one of the finest colored writers in the United States," was an author, poet, and lecturer. Born free in Toronto, Canada, after the Civil War, Mildred spent most of her adult life in Detroit. As the wife of William Lambert, a wealthy clothes dealer, political activist, and former abolitionist, she was an active member of the African-American political and social elites.

During the 1890s, as the editor of Detroit's *St. Matthew's Lyceum Journal*, Lambert was one of a few black women journalists, and among the most visible. Although its membership was small in comparison to that of the black Methodist and Baptist churches, St. Matthew's Protestant Episcopal Mission counted among its members nearly all of Detroit's black upper class. Thirty-one of the city's fifty-one families and individuals identified in the black social register were members of St. Matthews. Mildred Lambert's social position provided her with uncommon insights into the attitudes and practices of the social elite. Her writings demonstrate her class consciousness and concerns about racial unity.

"A Christmas Sketch" was published in the *Christian Recorder* in December 1882. Set in the early 1880s, this is a story about Ivy Varden, a beautiful mulatto and only child of wealthy parents who is thrust into poverty when her parents lose their fortune and die, leaving her penniless. Ivy, a resilient girl, is determined to find a job and to survive. Descending into poverty, she is shunned by her former friends. To support herself, she ekes out a living working as a governess and singing in a prominent church. Lambert suggests that Ivy is aware of less palatable options; that she could use her beauty to support herself by becoming the mistress of a married man or entering a life of prostitution. However, she asks God to help her "to do all to [reach] a pure and noble end."

Demonstrating that Christmas is a time for loving and sharing, Lambert shows how the love of a child can bring two people together. Ivy and Phillip Grey, two lonely people who would otherwise have spent Christmas Day alone, are brought together by the young Daisy, and their lives are forever changed.

Lambert uses Ivy to emphasize the class distinctions that existed in the black community. Although she describes Ivy's parents as wealthy, the definition of wealth in the black community has been relative to the economic status of African-Americans as a group. Historically, lifestyle differences between middle- and lower-class blacks have tended to be stark. In 1882, seventeen years after the abolition of slavery, there was a wide economic gap between blacks and whites and few African-Americans could lay claim to any degree of wealth. Mildred Lambert's position as a member of the black upper class provided her a unique vantage point to assess the particular tensions and issues that defined the individual and collective experiences of African-Americans, particularly black people in Detroit.

A Christmas Sketch

෨

"It came upon the midnight clear,
That glorious song of old.
From angels bending near the earth
To touch their harps of gold,

Peace on the earth, good will to men,
From heaven's all-gracious king;
The world in solemn stillness lay
To hear the angels sing."

With sweet and tender pathos the song is floating, filling every corner of a large and well attended church, in one of our most aristocratic thoroughfares. A vast concourse of fashionable people are standing spellbound beneath the fascinating influence of that glorious voice. Their strains of worship ceased with the soaring of those melting notes and the fair young creature by the side of the massive organ is bearing to God's throne the increase of scores of hearts in the pure burden of her song.

"Peace on earth, good will to men," and the head instinctively bows itself in reverence on every breast. The Amen is reached, the instrument throbbing and trembling, and the girlish figure sinks into a seat with a radiance on her pale features that makes the great dark eyes look as if they belonged to another sphere.

She is clad in deepest mourning and drawing her heavy veil over her face, its friendly shade hides from the outside world the hot tears that are falling thick and fast through her slender fingers.

Below, are the rich, the gay and the happy-hearted. Here and there she could discern well-remembered faces which she had known in happier days, but between whom and herself rose the inseparable barrier of poverty.

At last the great throng are leaving the edifice, and after watching the last of the number, she throws her veil aside from the tear-stained face and seats herself at the organ. Her frail fingers meander dreamily over the keys, now in plaintive cadence, now in soft winning melody, then suddenly rising, soaring, bursting, as it were, into a grand volume of sound, as the stately walls seemed to tremble with delight. She sees not a strange figure enter very near her, and sink crouching out of sight that her presence will not be observed when the young musician shall pass out.

There is a pause now, all the church within seems alive with the sweetest echoes of her grand anthems, as slowly and reverently she leaves the place.

How beautiful she is. How like a young priestess as she glides along unhesitatingly and seemingly so terribly alone, yet around the lovely mouth there is a sadness that makes the heart ache and the dear eyes seem indeed like "homes of silent prayer." She reaches her home, not amid the beautiful dwellings through which she has walked, but to an unpretending, yet respectable, humble street, and before a very modest looking house, where she unceremoniously enters. No glad voices bid her welcome, and she reaches her little room in silence, almost in gloom.

Pausing on the threshold she is surprised at the unusual stillness, for her beautiful bird has always greeted her with an outburst of song. The little fellow now [sits] on his perch shivering when she reaches in her hand and takes him with loving caress to her warm, loving breast.

"Ah, birdie, this is cold for you and me," she murmurs, "and our Christmas is sad indeed." The little fellow is very comfortable now, and he seems to take in the loneliness of his young mistress, for such a peal of song as he sends forth from his little throat seems to tell that there will be better days by and by.

She now gently replaces him and laying aside her wraps, her rich, dark, wavy hair, from which her comb has fallen, rolls down and about her, enveloping her slender form most gloriously. She stands there a creature of perfect loveliness, face to face with direst poverty—of *fare* and *friend*. God pity the beautiful Ivy, with thy fond heart reaching forth its sweet tendrils for love and friends and recoiling again more restless and longing than before. She thinks of the past, and the beautiful head sinks lower and lower on the breast. "Oh sorrow's crown of sorrow, remembering happier things."

Ivy Varden was the only child of wealthy parents whose first care ever was to guard their petted darling from the ills of life. She was reared in such tender consideration that one would naturally ignore the idea of the lovely blossom coming in contact with the rude, unfeeling world.

But there came a change, and in the period of life so full of beauty, and of love and joy, to tender, blooming girlhood, by one rude stroke all was swept away and life was now one deep, unfathomable shade. For a while the fond parents battled with fate, but soon under its privations and hardships, sank into death's dreamless rest, and Ivy was alone. She soon found that her fashionable friends were giving her the cold shoulder, which fact so stung her pride that she at once resolved to set their cold looks at defiance.

"I must *act*, I must *work*, I must *live*, and may God help me to do *all* to [reach] a pure and noble end."

She rented a little room, placed within the very barest necessaries of life and managed to be, in a measure, comfortable. She met with better success than she anticipated in obtaining employment as day governess in a few families among those of her former acquaintances.

She was an accomplished girl in every sense of the word, but if she excelled in any one thing more than another, it was music. In this she stood always among her associates in happier days without a rival. She also was only too glad to accept the position as soprano in one of the largest churches, and from the first effort hundreds would throng Sabbath after Sabbath, to drink in the melody of her wonderful voice. Today as her notes rang sweet and clear over the vast congregation, telling of peace and good will to man, none dreamed that the fair young creature had scarcely [anywhere] to lay her head.

"Miss Ivy, mamma wishes very much that you will come and eat dinner with us today, and I begged her so hard to let me come and bring you. Uncle Phil came last night and brought us lots of beautiful things, and I want you to come and see them. Will you come?"

Ivy raised her pale, tear-stained face toward the little speaker, who seemed as if she would never get to the end of mamma's message. She was about to refuse, but the earnestness and anxious expectation on the sweet little face compelled her at last to accept, so again donning her wraps she was soon walking rapidly to the great warm house by the side of the little prattler. The kind hearted lady was at the door to meet her.

"My dearest Ivy, how glad I am that you have not waited for

ceremony. I intended to have gone for you myself yesterday, but my brother arrived unexpectedly and I could not get away. He knew your dear papa well and wanted I should make him my messenger to fetch you hither."

All this while she bustled about the lonely girl, removing her things and drawing her to a great easy chair before the bright fire, seated herself beside her and tenderly sought to bring out the smiles from the young heart of her friend. She had succeeded well and Ivy's clear laugh was rippling forth, ringing out her charming dimples, and the great eyes looked like imprisoned stars, when the door opened and a tall handsome stranger entered the room.

"Oh, Uncle Phil, here is Miss Varden; she is just lovely; come and see for yourself."

"A very charming introduction, I am sure, my little chatterbox," then approaching Ivy [he] said with exquisite grace, "If we grown up people were allowed the perfect candor of childhood, I should feel that I were not presuming too much on my privileges as an old friend of your honored father, Miss Varden, by answering her question as my observation would fully allow me. I am sure I am proud and most happy to meet you."

"Your password into my very highest favor and esteem, Mr. Grey, was spoken at mention of dear papa's name. That you knew him and loved him, makes me feel that we are friends."

"A little child came into the world ages and ages ago, and brought into it life and joy and peace, and my little Daisy yonder, through her love prattlings for her 'beautiful Miss Ivy,' has given me more joy and happiness than I have known for years."

A shade of sadness swept over the noble face, and for a moment both were quiet until aroused by the pleasant voice of their hostess.

"Well, I thought you two people were going to mope away the Christmas hours. I shall have to send out for some one to come in and entertain you."

"Pray, do not think of it, sister mine. There are enough of us here and I promise you there shall be no more moping."

What a delightful day, after all. They talked and sang and played, until the day was lost in night shade, and the gay world was still. Phillip Grey thought there was not in the wide world one so beautiful a woman as Ivy Varden, while Ivy thought what a noble good man was Phillip Grey, and felt that she had known him for years.

As may be expected the rich, handsome bachelor was the delight of admiring mamas and the center of attraction to the adoring daughters, and of course, Ivy must be kept in the shade; and the little sisters were severely chastised for admiring her in their outspoken candor before the rich Mr. Grey, and when it was announced that the nuptials of this happy couple would be celebrated at a very early date, indignation knew no bounds and many were the maledictions hurled upon poor

Ivy's head. In Mr. Grey's presence, however, none dared breathe the name so dear to him save in most respectful terms.

One morning, after all the arrangements were completed for the wedding and departure, Ivy thought she would go over and have a parting with the grand old organ which had been such a source of comfort to her in lonely hours. How the sweet echoes stole through the silent edifice. How the great bursts of song seem to people the vast space with devout worshippers, then sinking into soft trembling melody where her glorious voice would glide in, making a most perfect harmony of sweetest sounds.

Suddenly a hand is laid upon her shoulder and Ivy is startled to find herself alone with the sad looking stranger. Her cheeks are wet, her frame trembles with her heart-sobbing.

"I know you will think me rude, young lady, but you are going away from here and I shall hear your sweet notes nevermore, but I wanted you to know how much good you have done me. Oh, if in all God's temples here on earth, such poor, sinful souls as mine are brought into his everlasting joy as you have had the power to do with me, your songs will mingle with the redeemed in the world of song."

Poor Ivy. Tears were falling with the poor creature's beside her.

For answer she turned and sang the same hymn she had sung on Christmas morn, when her life seemed so dark and alone, and when she had reached the beautiful verse.

O ye beneath life's crushing load,
Whose forms are bending low,
Who toil along the climbing way
With painful steps and slow,
Look now, for glad and golden hours
Come swiftly on the wing
O rest beside the weary road,
And hear the angels sing.

She raised her eyes and the poor creature had gone; but Phillip Grey stood now beside her with eyes full of tender love and moisture which he does not try to hide.

"Whatever of burden has been yours, my priceless love, may they be lost in my deep affection, and ever through the storms of life may we together listen and hear the angels sing."

Found After Thirty-Five Years—
Lucy Marshall's Letter—
A True Story for Christmas

∾

J. B. MOORE BRISTOR

J. B. Moore Bristor

Set in Virginia at Christmas, "Found After Thirty-Five Years—
Lucy Marshall's Letter" by Mrs. J. B. Moore Bristor was published in the *Christian Recorder* in December 1883. Like many
early black women writers, Bristor's biography remains hazy.
This particular story is the tale of two people, one white and one
black, whose families have been torn apart. The central characters are Mrs. Marshall, a white woman whose alcoholic husband
has brought the family to poverty, and Alfred Nelson, an illiter-
ate former slave, whose master sold him away from his mother at
the age of six. Alfred, a devoted father anguished over the recent
loss of his wife, contemplates placing his children in foster homes,
but decides to enlist Mrs. Marshall's aid in locating his family
members lost through the cruelty of the slave trade.

Alfred and Mrs. Marshall discover that although they are
separated by race, class, and gender, they are each struggling to
preserve their families, and that each in his own way can be of

help to the other. Mrs. Marshall takes great pride in writing and mailing the letters that help Alfred find his long-lost family. Seeing Alfred's strong commitment and loyalty to his family, Mrs. Marshall, after years of suffering verbal and mental abuse from her own husband, determines to face her problems and to take her children and leave him.

In this story, Mrs. J. B. Moore Bristor reflects upon the meaning and importance of Christmas as the time of Jesus Christ's birth, and his message to humanity that although we are beset with many problems, we must give of ourselves to others who also suffer. In the process of giving, she suggests that we as individuals are made whole.

Temperance, slavery, and gender issues are major subthemes in this story. Temperance, one of the most prominent of the nineteenth-century social-reform causes, was of great importance to both women and African-Americans. Alcohol was viewed as a destructive force operating against the individual and the family. Literature of the period constantly underscored women's ideal role as the keeper of morals, and emphasized their dependence on men. If the husband failed or the children did not turn out well, the woman was blamed. Women embraced the Temperance Movement as a means of maintaining stability in their homes and in their communities.

Bristor also focuses attention upon the brutality of slavery and demonstrates its impact on the black family while emphasizing that it can be possible for other formerly enslaved African-Americans to find their families. Like Alfred, after the Civil War there were many formerly enslaved African-Americans who searched for the families they had been so brutally separated from.

Alluding to some of the trials women of the time endured, Bristor speaks about the abuse that Mrs. Marshall received as a girl from her father and as a woman from her husband. In a subtle comparison of African-Americans and women, Marshall suggests that both are the victims of white male avarice. She raises the question "Would not a people that tolerated slavery, and now the rum traffic, legalize any outrage for gold?"

In the end, both Alfred and Mrs. Marshall achieve their goals, significantly because each of them has something to offer the other. Alfred, in his own way, is a role model of strength and courage for Mrs. Marshall. Mrs. Marshall, by sharing her knowledge and skills, helps Alfred find his mother and other family members and, in doing so, keep his children with his family.

Found After Thirty-Five Years—Lucy Marshall's Letter—A True Story for Christmas

∞

"Want any whitewashing done m'am?" asked Alfred Nelson, as he stood for a moment before a small Virginia house.

"If you can do good work you might undertake this room," answered an elderly woman. "Mrs. Marshall is out this morning, but I heard her say she only wanted an experienced hand, as the last man who did it made it look badly. Do you make a business of whitewashing?"

"I do whatever I can," was the answer. "My wife was [a] cook in the hotel, and lifting heavy things helped to bring on a cancer, the doctor says. She can't do anything now, and I have to pay a woman to take care of my three children."

Mrs. Marshall soon came in, and hearing Alfred's story, engaged him at once. She was a stranger in Virginia, having gone there after her marriage, which was a most unsuitable and unhappy one. Her husband had fine chances in life, but drank secretly, managing the habit so that it was hardly suspected in the church to which he belonged, its effects being felt by his family, to whom his laziness and drowsiness brought poverty. The house in which they lived, a plain brick, tastefully painted in Lucas' softest gloss shades, was mortgaged and now offered at Sheriff's sale. It had only two rooms down stairs, and three—one a mere cupboard in size—above, yet if the law had allowed Lucy Marshall the poor boon of quiet possession to herself, and liberty to work for her little ones in peace, undisturbed by Henry Marshall, she would have been thankful. Progress in some things has been made, but men are not far advanced in just treatment of women.

Mrs. Marshall was warm-hearted and felt for those who had been in bondage, and still suffered from ties that had been cruelly rent by so-called "owners." There were many colored people in the place, and she tried to help them. As she sat down to her work she asked Alfred if he had always been free.

"No, indeed," was his answer; "I lived in N— —, and was sold away from my mother when I was six years old, about thirty-six years ago [1847]." A shudder of horror passed through Mrs. Marshall as she asked:

"Did your mother see you taken away? How did it happen?"

"I was playing in the street, when my master came up and said:

"Alfred do you see that man on horseback?"

"I said yes, and he told me to go with him. He took me out of the place and I never saw or heard of any of my people again."

"Thirty-five years," repeated Mrs. Marshall. "Your mother is most likely dead or sold away, but some of your family might be there. Have you ever written to ask?"

"Yes, but I got no answer."

"It is worth trying again. I will write for you at any time, mind [you], and for any one else freely." She urged him that the letter should be written and sent there, but he did not seem much interested; in fact he had no change at that moment. Mrs. Marshall would offer it on what would be due him when the work was done, or give it, but she saw he chewed tobacco from time to time. Thrifty and [barely] managing herself, she felt less like offering, and after saying paper and envelope would be given, and the letter prepared at any time, she urged no more, her own perpetually recurring worries drawing off her attention. Alfred did his work and left. Spring, which only brought sadness to Mrs. Marshall, came and went, then summer and fall. December set in and things were darker than before. They were often on short allowance of food, though she turned everything to account, selling the plants in her neat garden raised from seeds and cuttings and accepting an offer at the lowest wages to review holiday books only during the illness of one of the editorial staff of a city paper.

The day was not very cold, and there was no fire save a small one lighted long enough to make a cup of coffee fresh and fragrant in the ideal pot that shone like silver. Then Lucy untied the parcels that had come by express, and turned over the tinted pages of some of Randolph's new books. In dainty bas relief was the "World's Christmas Hymn." Turning over the illustrations her eyes fell on the words:

> "The people are perplexed and saying,
>   How long? how long?
> And on my hand I bowed my head;
> There is no peace on earth, I said,
>   For hate is strong,
>   And mocks the song
> Of peace on earth, good will to men!
>
> Then pealed the bells more loud and deep;
> God is not dead, nor doth he sleep;
>   The wrong shall fail,
>   And mocks the song
> Of peace on earth, good will to men."

But to hear the words seemed a mockery just then. Why had her life been so? Why had she been brought to this place? She thought of those who had suffered in it more than she. If her heart quivered with anguish and was wild with rage and grief when brutal Henry Marshall threatened [that] if she left him [he would] take from her the infant that lay in the cradle, and hide him from her, how had other mothers felt whose children had been torn from them, and sold to a slavery worse than death? Would not a people that tolerated slavery, and now the rum traffic, legalize any outrage for gold? Mechanically she turned over other volumes, reading passages here and there. "The Appearances of Our Lord to Men before His Birth in Bethlehem" by Doctor Baker, who in Georgia remained at his post, standing loyal when those around him were false. She read over that page which speaks of Christ's having in almost every instance of healing, touched those whom he cured. "He laid his hand upon every one of them," is written of the multitude he healed. This was a type of human help and sympathy. But in those dreary years what had she known? And of all sufferers, I think few received less sympathy than the drunkard's wife. That men and women are now wakening to earnest efforts in temperance work is not so much from sympathy as their interest and fear. The nation did not rise in righteous indignation and put down slavery. Men waited till it became a political necessity, an absolute war measure, without which they could not conquer the foe. And not until the people see and realize that prohibition means economy in expense, low taxation, good times and prosperity, will it be carried. Meanwhile how long will be the heartache of weary wives and mothers.

"I have often found," said Lucy Marshall sadly to herself, "that in moments of deepest despair it is a good thing to try and help others. The year will close most sadly to me. Can I brighten it to some one else? When my work is done I shall go tonight to some of the cabins and offer to write for them."

That afternoon as she read Mrs. Prentiss' "Flower of the Family," remembering how she had first read it, years before in her girlhood, in days shadowed by ill treatment from an intemperate father, for the curse had come to her in more than one—yes more than two relations of life, she saw from the low window Alfred Nelson pass along the road. She lost no time calling him in.

"Alfred," she remarked, energetically, "I thought you told me you were coming back soon for me to write for you? Have you not waited long enough? How is your wife?"

"She is dead," was the answer.

Mrs. Marshall started. "And how are your children doing?"

"Oh, they are all going to live with different neighbors. One is to take one and one another; my wife knew that before she died." How quietly the man spoke for a change that would darken every young life!

"That is a sad prospect for them," was the reply. "More than ever should you try to find your mother or some of your family. I shall not wait for you [any] longer, but will write it myself. Did you not say you had written once and got no answer?"

"Yes," said Alfred, "I wrote twice."

"To whom?"

"To my old master."

"You did not, surely," was the amazed answer. "Could you suppose that any man who would be vile enough to sell a child from his mother, would answer you and let you know anything that would be of comfort to you?"

"Yes, I thought he would," said Alfred.

"Then I think you are simple," was Lucy's answer, as she wrote down the names of master, Alfred's mother, brother and family, giving the circumstances of his going away. She directed this letter to the ministers of the Methodist and Baptist churches for colored people in the place he had once lived, and begged them to read it out for a number of Sabbaths in succession morning and night, and ask the people to inquire. A stamped envelope was also enclosed.

Alfred went away hardly seeming as much interested as Mrs. Marshall.

Henry was more outrageous than usual that week, and Mrs. Marshall cast over every project in her agonized mind and resolved to face all and leave him. It was no fit place to bring up children. Such language would soon corrupt them. How her head ached that winter morning as she walked to the village post office, receiving her own yellow envelope returned in wonderfully quick time from the Virginia village. She could hardly credit the contents. Alfred's mother was in church when the letter was read, and his brother wrote that when in the Union Army as a soldier he had inquired for him every place he went, but could hear nothing. He was to come on at once and bring the children; they would take care of them.

"My way indeed has been dark," said Lucy, "but perhaps for this God brought me here. At any rate before I leave I will try and lighten other hearts." Out of a number of efforts, one other succeeded.

Alfred did not leave for some time and was at first influenced by some persons for whom he worked for very low wages, who were unwilling to lose him. But at last he went with the orphans, writing back that his mother was almost wild with joy. Lucy did not say that her inefficient son was a little afraid [to leave]; he might have to help her, and it turned out that all were ready and willing to help [her].

Dear friend, my story is true, all save names, and I doubt not that it is possible for some of you to meet long parted friends, or at least hear of them by pursuing the same means. Is it not worth any cost or repeated effort?

The Blue and the Gray

❧

AUGUSTUS M. HODGES

Augustus M. Hodges

Augustus Michael Hodges, a noted journalist and fiction writer, had a predilection for writing Christmas stories. In addition to "The Blue and the Gray," he was the author of "The Christmas Reunion Down at Martinsville," "The Prodigal Daughter: A Story of Three Christmas Eves," "Three Men and a Woman," and "Three Christmas Eves."

Hodges was born in Williamsburg, New York, on March 18, 1854. A graduate of the Hampton Normal and Industrial Institute, he went on to distinguish himself as a politician, journalist, and fiction writer. Like his illustrious father Willis A. Hodges, a pioneering journalist and abolitionist, Hodges dedicated his life to fighting racism and bigotry. In 1876 he was elected to the Virginia House of Delegates, where he served one term. In the early 1890s his candidacy for the position of U.S. Minister to Haiti received the endorsement of over five hundred leading Republicans. Failing to receive the appointment he continued to write and publish fiction and serve as a columnist for several black and white newspapers and periodicals, including the *Indianapolis Freeman* and *Baltimore Afro-American.* In 1890 he established *The Brooklyn Sentinel,* which for three years was considered one of the leading African-American newspapers in New York State. In 1894, with the support of several other literary figures, he formed the Augustus M. Hodges Literary Syndicate to publish black fiction. During the late nineteenth and early twentieth centuries the *Indianapolis Freeman* purchased many of his short stories from this organization.

"The Blue and the Gray," similar to most of Hodges's short stories, recalls African-American tradition and experience, which enables his writing to assume a historical dimension. Hodges wrote about social problems and real people. However, he did so in a careful and ritualistic manner that allowed the inclusion of both myth and symbol. Exploring racial identity and conflict, he typically interjected historical events, names, places, and quotes into his fiction. He prided himself on writing stories that were bound "by facts, not fiction." Hodges's realistic fiction frequently contrasted patterns of life and issues of race as reflected in the South and the North and rural and urban America. He also distinguished middle- and upper-class black life from that of the deprived and struggling working classes. In doing so, he utilized period stereotypes, which invariably depicted Northern cities as dens of vice and destruction, filled with anguished characters devoid of feeling.

Published in the *Indianapolis Freeman* in December 1900, "The Blue and the Gray," as its title indicates, is a reflection upon the Civil War and the issue of race central to that struggle. Hodges's intention is to explore the aftermath of the war and demonstrate the need for racial healing. He alludes to the discrimination that existed in the Grand Army of the Republic (GAR), an organization of Civil War veterans founded in the late 1860s. Once bitter enemies, by the 1890s white Union and Confederate soldiers bonded together in their efforts to exclude and segregate black veterans, members of the GAR.

The plot, set in the mid-1890s, revolves around Thomas Wright and Jack Nash, whose paths cross as young soldiers fighting on opposite sides during the Civil War, and, much later, as old men leading marginal lives in New York City. Hodges demonstrates how Wright, an embittered and lonely African-American who had been cheated out of his earnings by whites and blacks, males and females, recovers his sense of humanity through relating to the suffering of another person, Nash.

In "The Blue and the Gray," Hodges, an ardent integrationist, uses the Christmas theme to stress the need for racial understanding. He reinforces the idea that the racial divide can be bridged and that there is hope for the races. Hodges's optimism was articulated at a time when African-American men had been disfranchised, racial stereotyping and lynching were rampant, and walls of legal segregation were being erected in all areas of American life.

The Blue and the Gray

୭୬

Chapter I

"'Twas the night before Christmas, and all through the house," with one exception, everything was life, noise and hurry. The house was a large fashionable colored boarding house on West 21st street, New York City, over which Mrs. Sarah Brink presided. The house was indeed "up side down," as most of the boarders were leaving, or had left to spend the holidays out of town with friends. Expressmen were calling for trunks and bags. Messenger boys were bringing and taking away presents, and grocery and market men were leaving goods for the Christmas dinner. Mrs. Brink was going to give [gifts] to a few select friends and the few boarders who were not invited out to dine. The good lady and her three daughters were figuratively speaking, "up to their eyes" in flour and dough. The only part of the house where there was no cheer, expectation or preparation, was in the front basement, which Mrs. Brink had rented out to an old bachelor, who, her youngest daughter termed "a miserly old crank of a beggar."

Old Tom Wright sat silently by his fire smoking his [pipe], perhaps thinking of better days, and perhaps not thinking at all. Miss Eva Brink said the old man had lived in the basement for five years, during which time he had hardly spoken to any one in the house excepting his landlady. When he paid her his one dollar and a quarter room rent every Monday morning he would growl out "Good morning; give me a receipt, please;" halt, snatch the same and walk out to his work. When any of the boarders met him coming in, or going out, and greeted him with "Good morning" or "Good afternoon," he grunted out a reply, the translation of which was left to the imagination of the hearer. As there were several ladies in the house besides the boarding house keeper and her three daughters, the opinions of, and rumors about "the old crank in the cellar" (as they were pleased to call the basement dweller), must have kept the old man's ears at a white heat. Some said he had run away from his wife and family; some said he was a woman hater; some [said] that he had lots of money; others that he had none. In fact all kinds of comments ten or a dozen women can make about a man, when they get together for daily gossip, were daily made.

The fact of the matter was [that] old Tom Wright was a misan-thropist—can you blame him? Twenty odd years before this story begins he went to New York from Macon, [Georgia,] homeless, friendless, and unknown. After a year, or so, of untold hardships, he found employment as a porter for a wholesale leather house, in that business portion of the town known as "the swamp." He was in the firm's employ for nearly thirty years. He worked hard the first ten years and saved almost every dollar he earned; then a "slick" young white man buncoed him out of the money. He saved again for several years, when a colored man got his earnings out of the bank on a forged check. His last boarding house mistress robbed him out of a few hundred dollars. The last of the milk of human kindness was dried up, just before he took up his abode at Mrs. Brink's, when his pocket was picked at a church funeral. Can we blame him for hating all humanity; big, little, black, white, male and female? He was now a broken down, old man—not the fine, strong, six foot, young full blooded Negro of thirty years prior—on half pay at the store. [He was] kept on the pay roll out of pure charity, on account of his being "a good old has been;" a fact the old man felt keenly. He lived secluded from the world, and never went out, save now and then to church on Sunday evening. The few dollars he now had, he was saving up to buy a bed in the Aged Colored People's Home in Brooklyn, where he could spend the rest of his days without the fear of a poor house. We forgot to state that the old man was a "property holder." Yes, he bought at a great sacrifice a small plot of ground—in Cypress Hills Cemetery—a small plot just large enough for two. The reason he bought a double plot was because it was the smallest they would sell and fence in. Here he hoped to sleep his last sleep. Having thus prepared for himself, he took little interest in the cold world's doings, and was deaf to the noise and bustle of his neighbors up stairs.

Suddenly [one night] about eight o'clock, everything and everybody in the house got quiet. The stillness seemed to arouse old Tom Wright. He jumped to his feet, looked out of the window, and remarked to himself aloud: "Well, its Christmas Eve; guess I'll go out and buy a small turkey and fixings, and have a Christmas dinner by myself. It may be the last one." He went to a book shelf, ran his finger along a row of books until he came to a certain one, pulled it out and took a five dollar bill from between its leaves, put it in his pocket, put on his hat and coat and went over to 7th Avenue, where he bought a small turkey, and the needful "trimmings," and started home.

The streets were full of people, half of whom in that section were colored. They were going here and there, the good, bad and indifferent. Lots of professional beggars were out wishing every one who gave them a coin, "a merry Christmas," and those who refused, a warm seat in a hot place in the hereafter.

An old white man in rags, with white locks, stood on the corner of 7th Avenue, and 30th Street, with extended hand asking for help—a few pennies to get a bed for the cold night. Every one, black and white, passed him by; (the average New Yorker's ears are deaf to the cries of the tramp and professional beggar). Still, even New Yorkers can make mistakes, as the old man was, in reality an object for charity. "Say Boss!" "Hey Capt!" "Kind Lady!" "Young Fellow!" "Dear Boy!" and "For Heaven's Sake Friend, please give me a dime to get a bed for the night," did not reach either the hearts or pocket books of the passers by. "What will I say?" thought the old man, as Tom Wright, a man as old as himself, came up. "Comrade," he replied to himself. "Hey, there, Comrade! will you help an old soldier, like yourself, to a dime to keep him from camping out tonight? Ain't you an old soldier?" he asked old Tom.

"Yes, but not a Grand Army [of the Republic] man; I never joined the Grand Army, so go to them," said old Tom.

"I am not a Grand Army man either, but I'm a [veteran] of the Civil War, and got scars on my breast to prove it too."

"So have I. Come home with me, I will give you shelter for the night, and a Christmas dinner."

After getting the old soldier "something to warm him up," old Tom Wright took him to his room and fixed a bed for him. Tom's heart had resumed its normal condition towards suffering humanity, for the time being anyway. After the warm supper his guest said: "Now I'll peel off [my clothes] and show you the scar I got from a fellow on the other side, during the Civil War," and he started to pull off his half of a shirt.

"Yes, and I will show the slice cut out of my shoulder by an old Rebel," replied old Tom Wright, as he started to remove his shirt.

In a minute the two men stood shirtless before each other. Their eyes met; each recalled the scar upon the other; each knew that he had inflicted the scar upon which he gazed.

*"The things we wish to be, we are
For one transcendent moment."*

For a moment the two old men, once six feet in height, stood erect and were young again, once more, one with a black face and blue uniform, the other [with a] white face and gray uniform, confronted each other as they did on the battle field thirty years before. It was only a moment, [before] age drew them back to the size of two old men — three score and ten. They smiled, and at the same time extended hands. "So it's you, Reb?" asked old Tom.

"Yes Nig it's me," said his guest.

"Well," replied Tom, "we are too old to fight now. Let's go to bed, and tomorrow we will eat a Christmas dinner at the reunion of two of the best hand to hand fighters who wore the blue and gray during the war." The next day these two old "vets," who nearly killed each other in a hand to hand combat, dined together in peace.

Chapter II

It was on the morning of April 12th, 1864, that the Rebel General Forrest suddenly appeared before Fort Pillow, located a few miles below Memphis[, Tennessee]. The fort, was in part garrisoned, by a colored troop, the 6th U.S. heavy artillery, of which Thomas Wright, a six foot, full blooded Negro, was a brave and faithful corporal. Major Booth commanding the Union troops at Fort Pillow, received from Major General Forrest, the rebel leader, the following:

Headquarters of Forrest Cavalry Corps,
Paducah, [Kentucky] April 12th, 1864.

To Major Booth, commanding the Federal forces at Fort Pillow:

"Having an ample force sufficient to carry your works and reduce the fort, in order to avoid the unnecessary effusion of blood, I demand the surrender of the fort. If you comply, the white prisoners will be treated as prisoners of war; [and] the blacks [will be] returned to their masters. But, if I have to storm your works, you may expect no quarter."

"N. B. FORREST,
Maj. Gen. Commanding."

Major Booth declined to surrender, and Forrest's massacre at Fort Pillow became a historic fact. The garrison fled pell mell only to be overtaken and murdered by wild rebels. One of the men, who resolved to sell his life as dearly as possible, was Corporal Wright. With a yell, and [an] uplifted knife, Jack Nash, a young rebel, [Wright's] size and weight, rushed at him. Wright drew his pistol and shot the fellow in the thigh. His foe fell as he was running backwards. Wright also fell forward. The two men were within reach of each other. They clinched in the fight of death; both drew their knives. The black man, in blue, cut a deep crescent shaped piece of flesh out of the breast of his foe. The white man, in gray, cut off the fleshy part of his foe's shoulder, and bit off his left thumb. They fought, and rolled over and over, until both became unconscious. When they came to themselves the next day, they were both in the Union hospital, miles away from Fort Pillow on cots, side by side, where human northern nurses had brought them back to life. Their eyes met, and both swore to kill the other the first time they met, if they lived. "Hey Nig, if I get out of here I'll finish you," said the man in gray, to which the man in blue replied:

"I'll finish cutting your heart out Reb, if I have to follow you all over the world for a hundred years." "Nig" and "Reb" were the names they called each other every day when they had occasion to speak to each other. At last they were pronounced well and both shipped to their homes [each] without knowing the whereabouts of the other. It was thirty years before they met again as old men in New York City and ate Christmas dinner as friends.

Tom Wright offered to share his home with his old foe and the homeless old fellow accepted the offer. Wright's firm went out of business that New Year's day, but he had enough to keep him and his new friend from want. Three days before the following Christmas, old Jack Nash, the man who wore the gray, died of pneumonia, and was buried in Tom Wright's plot. Tom Wright joined the [Grand Army of the Republic], to whom he told the story. When he died last year they placed the man who wore the blue beside the man who wore the gray.

In the northeast corner of Cypress Hill Cemetery, on a hill called "Mount Hope" can be seen the resting place of these two old soldiers. A fitting monument tells the romantic story.

"Black and White, in Blue and Gray, Sleeping together till judgment day."

The Test of Manhood:
A Christmas Story

ಞ

PAULINE ELIZABETH HOPKINS

Pauline Elizabeth Hopkins

"The Test of Manhood" was written by Pauline Elizabeth Hopkins, one of the most prolific and important black writers to emerge at the turn of the century, and published under the nom de plume "Sarah A. Allen," her mother's maiden name. Her interest in theater and African-American history is manifest in her early work as a playwright and actress, and in her extensive and diverse writings. Born in Portland, Maine, in 1859, and raised in Boston, Hopkins was the scion of a prominent black middle-class family. A keen observer of black life and culture, she believed that black writers must use fiction to tell the story of African-American life and history. As the literary editor of the Boston-based *Colored American Magazine*, one of the first African-American journals to offer black writers an open forum for expression, Hopkins became known as one of its major contributors. The majority of her short stories, biographical sketches of black historical figures, and serialized novels appeared in the *Colored American Magazine* between 1900 and mid-1904.

Hopkins's fiction, particularly her novels, tended to focus on the black Southern elite and upper middle class, but many of her short stories center on the life of the working class. In addition to "The Test of Manhood," Hopkins wrote several Christmas stories, including "Bro'r Abr'm Jimson's Wedding" and "General Washington."

"The Test of Manhood," published in the December 1902 issue of the *Colored American Magazine,* is, perhaps, a spin-off or a prelude to her novel, *Contending Forces,* published in 1900. In both writings, Hopkins explores the issue of skin color. Hopkins focuses on the color line in "The Test of Manhood" and depicts how it divides blacks and whites into separate but unequal worlds, and also how it separates and causes particular anguish in members of the same family.

The principal character in "The Test of Manhood," Mark Myers, is a mulatto who leaves his black mother in the South and passes for white in the North. As Myers rises to wealth and status, Hopkins shows that to pass for white was living a lie and inviting unforeseen tragedy with possibly destructive consequences. The "passing" theme emphasized in "The Test of Manhood" also appears in the Harlem Renaissance novels of Nella Larsen, James Weldon Johnson, and Jessie Fauset.

The Test of Manhood: A Christmas Story

෨

The shed door creaked softly, and Mark Myers stood for a moment peering into the semi-darkness of the twilight. He was a stalwart lad of about eighteen, with soft dark curls, big dark eyes, and the peach-like complexion of a girl, but he was only a Negro, what the colored people designate as "milk an' molasses, honey; neither one thing nor t'other." And he was leaving his home to try his fortune at the North.

One day Mark had carried a white gentleman's bag to the steamboat landing and as he loitered about the pier after pocketing a generous fee, the words of the patron in conversation with another white man sank in his heart:

"After all this wasted blood and treasure, the Negro question is still uppermost in the South. Why don't you settle it once and for all, Morgan?"

"We might were it not for the infernal interference of you Yankees, and amalgamation. The mulattoes are the curse of the South. We can't entirely ignore our brothers' cousins and closer kindred, so there you are."

"Your brothers and closer kindred could settle the question themselves if they knew their power."

"How?" queried Morgan.

"Easily enough; when the white blood is pronounced enough, just disappear and turn up again as a white man. Half of your sectional difficulties would end under such a system."

"And would you—a white man—be willing to encounter the risk that such a course would entail—the wholesale pollution of our race?" thundered the man called Morgan, in disgust.

"Why not? You know the old saw,—Where ignorance is bliss 'tis folly to be wise. Better that than a greater evil."

"You Northerners are a riddle—"

They passed out of sight and Mark heard no more, but from that time he had thought incessantly of the stranger's words, and at last he resolved to become a white man. And one night when his mother lay peacefully sleeping, with no foreshadowing of the sorrow in store for her, with a backward look of regret and a tear stealing down his cheek, he had stolen softly from the little cabin under the wide spreading magnolia. At the top of the hill he paused for a last look and then turned his face sorrowfully toward the great unknown world, henceforth to be his only home. The day broke; the sun rose; there was a stir of life all about him. How sweet the air smelled; surely there could be no prettier morning up in the wonderful North to which he was journeying.

As he trudged along with his small bundle over his shoulder he murmured to himself: "Mammy's up now, but she won't miss me yet. I'm glad I chopped all that wood yesterday. It ought ter last her a week an' better. The white folks all think the world of her. They'll take keer on her tell I git settled; then I'll write and tell her all about my plans."

He avoided the main roads and kept to the fields, thus keeping clear of all chance acquaintances who might interfere with his determination to identify himself with the white race.

The weary time passed on: days were merged into weeks, when one morning tired and fainting with hunger, Mark found himself in the street of a great Northern metropolis, homeless and nearly penniless. He walked through the thoroughfares with the puzzled uncertainty of a stranger doubtful of his route, pausing at intervals to study the signs, feeling his heart sink as he watched the hurrying throng of unfamiliar faces. The scene was so different from his beautiful southern home that in his heart he cried aloud for the dear familiar scenes. Then he remembered and took up his weary tramp again and his search for a friendly face that he might venture to accost the owner for work. Night was approaching and he must have a place to sleep. As he neared the common, and its tranquil, inviting greenness burst upon his view, he determined that if nothing better presented itself, to pass the night there under the canopy of heaven.

As he neared Tremont street a gentleman passed him, evidently in a great hurry. Scarcely had his resounding footsteps ceased upon the concrete walk, when Mark noticed a pocket-book lying directly at his feet. He picked it up, opened it and saw that it was filled with bills of large denominations. "John E. Brown" was printed in gold letters upon one of the compartments.

Mark stood a second hesitating as to the right course to pursue: here was wealth—money for food, shelter, clothes—he sighed as he thought of what it would give him. But only for a moment, the next he was rushing along the wide mall at his utmost speed trying to overtake the gentleman whom he could just discern making his hurried way through the throng of pedestrians.

At the corner of Summer and Washington streets, Mark, breathless and hatless, caught up with the gentleman.

"Eh, what? My pocket-book?" ejaculated Mr. Brown, as he felt in all his pockets, and looked down curiously upon the forlorn figure that had tugged so resolutely at his arm to attract his attention.

"Now that was clever of you and very honest, my boy," said the great lawyer, gazing at him over his gold-rimmed spectacles. "Here's something for you," and he placed a bill in the lad's hand that fairly made the dark eyes bulge with surprise. "From the country, aren't you?"

"Yes, sir."

"I thought so. Honesty doesn't flourish in city air. Well, I haven't time to talk to you today. Come to see me tomorrow at my office, perhaps I can help you. Want a job don't you?"

"Yes, sir; I'm a stranger in Boston."

"Come and see me, come and see me. I'll talk with you, Good-day."

The lawyer went on his way. In one brief moment the world to Mark seemed spinning around. His breath came in quick struggling gasps, while wild possibilities surged through his brain, when he read the card in his hand which was that of a firm of lawyers whom he had often heard spoken of even in his far-off home.

The next morning Mark presented himself at the office and was kindly received by Mr. Brown. The lawyer glanced him over from head to foot. "A good face," he thought, "and pleasant way." Then he noted the neat, cheap suit, the well-brushed hair and clean-looking skin. Then he asked a few direct, rapid questions, which Mark answered briefly.

"What can you do?"

"Plow, make a garden an'—an' read and write," dropping his voice over the two last accomplishments.

The lawyer laughed heartily.

"What's your name?"

"Mark Myers, sir."

"Well, Mark, I like your face, and your manner, too, my lad, and although it's contrary to my way of doing—taking a boy without reference—because of your honesty you may set in as a porter and messenger here. If you've a mind to try the job, we want a boy just now, so you see you have struck it just right for yourself and me, too."

"If you are willing to take me, sir just as you find me, I will do my best to please you," answered Mark, controlling his voice with an effort.

"Well, then, we'll consider it a bargain. I'll pay you what you are worth."

As Mark stepped across the threshold of the inner office and hung up his hat and coat he felt himself transformed. He was no longer a Negro! Henceforth he would be a white man in very truth. After all his plans, the metamorphosis had been accomplished by fate. For the first time he seemed to live—to feel.

That night, he sat motionless beside the open window of the garret where he had found lodging and planned his future.

"Oh, mammy," he cried at last, "if you knew, you would forgive me. Some day you shall be rich—" He broke off suddenly and dropped his head in his hands. Did he mean this, he asked himself in stern self-searching. His mother could not be mistaken for a white woman—her skin was light, but her hair and features were those of a Negress. He shuddered at the gulf he saw yawning between them. Nothing could bridge it. From now on she should no more exist—as his mother—for he had buried his old self that morning, and packed the earth hard above the coffin.

As the months went by a curious change came to the lad. This new life—this masquerade, so to speak, had become second nature. He looked at life from a white man's standpoint, and had assumed all of the prejudices and principles of the dominant race. Out of the careless boy had come a wary, taciturn man. He availed himself of the exceptional school privileges offered by night study in Boston, and improved rapidly. One morning, Mr. Brown came to Mark with good news. He had promoted him from porter to clerk, with a corresponding increase in his salary.

That night, Mark dreamed he was at home with his mother. He felt the loving touch of her toil-worn dusky hands, and heard the caressing tones of her voice in its soft Southern dialect. Ah! there had been such infinite peace in the old, careless, happy life he had led there. Pictures came and went before his mental vision with startling distinctness. He saw the modest log-cabin, the sweet-scented magnolia-tree, the cotton fields, the sweeping long, gray moss hanging from the trees, the smell of the pines; he heard the cow-bells in the cane-break, the hum of bees, and the sweet notes of the mocking-bird. He closed his eyes and could see the boys and girls dancing the old "Virginia reel:"

> "Dar's 'Jinny Put de Kittle On,' an' 'Shoo!
> Miss Pijie, Shoo!'
> An' den 'King William Was King George's
> Son,'

'Blin' Man's Bluff,' an' 'Gimme Korner'; also
    'Walk de Lonesum Road,'
'Whar de pint wuz gittin kisses —shorz yo'
    born,
De gals wuz dressed in hum'spun, long wid
    dar brogan shoes,
An' ef dar feet would tech yo,' you would feel,
'Do' de boys wore bed-tuck breeches, dese
    trifles wuz forgot,
While 'joyin' ub de ol' Virginny reel."

After that night he resolutely put by such thoughts; all his associates were white, and his life was irrevocably blended with the class far above the humble blacks. Months rounded into years. At the end of five years, Mark was on the road to wealth. He had studied law and passed the Bar. A fortunate speculation in Western land was the motive power that placed ten thousand dollars in his pocket.

"So unexpected a windfall might have ruined some men," Mr. Brown confided to his partner as they smoked an after dinner cigar at Parker's, "but no fear for Mark. His is an old head on young shoulders. He's bound to be a power in the country before he dies."

"How about a 'Co.,' Brown? ever thought of it in connection with the firm? We aren't growing any younger. What do you think of it?"

"Just the thing, Clark, Co. it is; and Myers is the man."

The winter had set in early that year. Snow covered the ground from the first of December. The air was biting cold. The music of sleigh-bells mingled with the voices of children playing in the streets. There was good skating on the frog pond and the Public Garden, where the merry skaters glided to and fro in graceful circles laughing and jesting merrily.

Down in the quarter where the colored people lived, Aunt Cloty sat most of the day looking drearily through the rusted iron railings of the area in a hopeless watch for a footstep that never came. Old, wrinkled, rheumatic, the patient face, and subdued air of the mulattress awakened sad feelings in the hearts of those who knew her story.

She had come North five years before searching for her son. At first she had been able to live in a humble way from her work as a laundress, but when sickness and old age laid their hands upon her, she had succumbed to the inevitable and subsisted upon the charity of the well-to-do among her neighbors, who had something to spare for a companion in poverty. After a time her case had come under the notice of the associated charities. At first it was determined to place the helpless creature in an institution where she could have constant attention, but her prayers and tears not to be "kyarted to de po'-house," had stirred the pity of the officials and at length the attention of lawyer Brown's daughter Katherine had been directed to Aunt Cloty as a worthy object of charity. Miss Brown was delighted with the quaintness of the old Negress and her tender heart overflowed with pity for her woes, and so the helpless woman became a welcome charge upon the purse of the petted favorite of fortune. Since that time better days had dawned for Aunt Cloty.

The wealthy girl and the old mulattress grew to be great friends. Every week found Katherine visiting her protege, sitting in the tiny room, listening eagerly to her tales of the sunny South.

Aunt Cloty's turban always seemed the insignia of her rank and proud pretensions, for she declared there was "good blood" in her veins, and her majestic bearing testified to the truth of her words. When Cloty felt particularly humble, she laid the turban in flat folds on her head. In her character of a laundress, it was mounted a little higher. But when she received visitors, or called an enemy to account, the red flag of defiance towered aloft in wonderful proportion. So, "Miss Katherine" could always read the signs of her protege's feelings in the build of the red turban.

Christmas week the turban lay in flat folds and Cloty mourned aloud.

"He mus' be daid. 'Deed, chile, he mus' be daid or he'd neber leave his ol' mammy to suffer," she cried as she rocked her frail body in the old wooden rocker. "Miss Katherine" sat patiently listening.

"You see, Missie, Sonny's da onlies' chile what I ebber had. De good Lawd sent him to me lak He done Isaac to Sary, in my ole age, an' sence de night he runned off I aint seed nuffin' but trouble. All dat fust ye'r I was spectin' him back again, an' when de win moan roun' my cabin endurin' o' de night, it seemed lak I hear him callin' fer me, an' I git up an open de do' ter listen, but it waz dark an' lonesome an' he wazn't dar. So, at las' Marse Will, he sez ter me (Marse Will's one o' my white fokes, whar I dunn nurse for two ginerations, an' he call me mammy same as Sonny do,) — so Marse Will he sez to me, 'Mammy, Sonny's daid, or else he'd a written you whar he was. Sonny is allers been a good boy, an' he wouldn't act no sech way as this to you ef he was livin.' Yes, Missie, dats what Marse Will, he tell me, an' it suttinly did seem reasonable, but somehow I cayn't b'lieve it." She paused, and opening an old carpet-sack always laid by her chair on the floor, drew from it a package. "Dis here is his leetle red waist an' de fus' par' o' britches he ebber wo'," she continued, displaying them to the young white girl with pride. "I fotch um Norf wif me kaze dey keeps me company up here all alone."

Missie Katherine's swimming eyes attested her sympathy.

"He wuz de pertes' youngster," continued the old woman, with an upward tilt of her turbaned head, "an' de day he put dese on he strut, Missie, same as er peafowil."

"Aunt Cloty, I've told my father of your son and he's going to institute a search for him. If he's alive he'll find him for you, rest assured of that."

"Gord bless you, honey; Gord bless you. A big gentleman like de judge, your pa 'll surely fin' him, fer I b'lieve Sonny's alive somewhere.

Does I wanter see him?" and the woman's faded eyes held a joyous sparkle. "Does I wanter see him? Why honey," coming close to the girl and unconsciously grasping her arm, "ef he was in prison, an' I couldn' git ter him no urrer way I'd be willin' to crawl on my hands and knees ez fur agin ez I done come to git up Norf, jes' fur one look at him." For a moment she looked about her as though dazed, then some over-strained chord seemed to snap, and burying her face in her apron she sobbed aloud.

"Now, Aunty, don't," and the impulsive heiress threw her arms about the forlorn figure and kissed the wrinkled face. "Tomorrow is Christmas-eve, and I am coming for you early in the day to take you home. You are to live with me always after that, and if we don't find Sonny, you shall never want while I live."

"I's hearn tell of fokes cryin' kase dey's happy, but I aint neber done it tell now. Ef I kin jes fin' Sonny I'll be de happies' old woman in de whole wurl."

And so it came about that Aunt Cloty was domiciled in the home of Judge Brown.

Christmas-eve in a great city is a wonderful sight. The principal streets were in grand illumination. The shop windows were all ablaze, and through them came the vivid coloring of holiday gifts, tinting the cold-ness with an idea of warmth. It was a joyous pleasant scene; the pavements were thronged, and eager traffic was going on. A band of colored street musicians were passing from store to store stopping here and there to sing their peculiar songs to the accompaniment of guitars, banjos, and bones. One trolled out in a powerful bass the notes of the old song:

> *"The sun shines bright in my old Kentucky*
> *home,*
> *'Tis summer the darkies are gay."*

The familiar air fell upon the ears of a handsome dark-eyed man as he took his way leisurely through the throng. He paused a moment, dropped a coin in the hat extended for contributions, laughed, and hastened on his way. Presently he hummed the strain he had just heard in a rich undertone. Then there floated through his mind the fragments of a poem he had read somewhere:

> *"Hundreds of stars in the pretty sky;*
> *Hundreds of shells on the shore together;*
> *Hundreds of birds that go singing by;*
> *Hundreds of bees in sunny weather.*

> *"Hundreds of dewdrops to greet the dawn;*
> *Hundreds of lambs in the purple clover;*

Hundreds of butterflies on the lawn;
But only one mother the wide world over!"

"Pshaw!" exclaimed Mark Myers as he pulled himself together and brushed aside unpleasant memories.

Katherine Brown had been walking restlessly up and down the great reception room. The sound of the bell reached her. She stopped a moment, held her breath and listened. She heard Mark's voice in the hall and knew that her lover had come.

The servants were moving about in the back room, so she closed the folding doors, and hid the Christmas tree, and sat down demurely waiting for him to come in, as if she had not indulged in a thought about the matter until then; though her heart was beating so tumultuously that a tuft of flowers among the lace on her bosom fluttered as if a breeze passed over it. The dainty room was redolent with the perfumes from a basket of tea-roses, Japan lilies and japonicas that had been sent to the lovely girl as her first Christmas gift in the morning. Their fragrance pervaded the whole room, and it seemed that the fair owner moved through the calm of a tropical climate when she came forward to receive her guest; for that portion of her dress that swept the floor was rich with lace and summer-like in its texture, as if the blast of a storm could never reach her.

"My darling, you scarcely expected me, I am sure," said Myers coming forward with hand extended and a world of love-light in his dark eyes: "but nothing would keep me from you tonight, foolish fellow that I am."

"I should never have forgiven you if you had not come," replied the girl with arched tenderness. "Why, sir I have waited a half-hour already."

"Wondering what I should bring you for a Christmas gift?"

"No, no—not that," she answered, turning her eyes on the basket of flowers and blushing like a rose. "That came this morning, and I would let them put nothing else in this room, for your roses turned it into a little heaven of my own."

"They will perish in a day or two at best. But I have really brought you something that will keep its own as long as we two shall love each other."

"So long! Then it will be perfect to all eternity."

Mark grew serious. Something in her words struck him with a thought of death; a chill passed over him.

"God forbid that it should not remain so while you and I live, Katherine; for see, it is the engagement-ring I have brought you."

A flood of crimson rose to her face. The little hand held out for the ring quivered like a leaf. She held the star-like solitaire in her hand a moment gazing on it with reverence, scarcely conscious of its beauty. It might have been a lot of glass rather than a limpid diamond for anything she thought of the matter, she only felt how solemn and sacred a thing that jewel was.

"No, you must put it on first," she said, resting one hand softly on his breast, and holding the ring toward him. "I shall always love it better if taken from your own fingers."

Myers gazing down into her face, read all the solemn and beautiful thoughts that prompted the action, and his own sympathetic nature was subdued by them into solemn harmony.

As he stood before her submitting one hand to her sweet will, he whispered: "And you are happy, my beloved?"

"Happy! Oh, Mark, if we could always be so, heaven would begin here with you. Nothing can part us now, we are irrevocably bound to each other forever. If only the whole world could be happy as we are tonight."

Her words jarred upon him an instant. His old mother's face rose before him as it had not done for years.

"Come," said Katherine, "let me show you the Christmas tree; they—papa and Aunt Cloty—are just finishing it."

As she spoke she threw wide the doors and in the midst of the glitter and dazzle he heard a voice scream out:

"Oh, my Gord! It's him! It's my boy! It's Sonny!"

Then panting excitedly, arms extended, the yellow face suffused with tenderness, Mark saw his mother standing before him.

After that scream came a deathly silence, Mark stood as if carved into ruins, Katherine lost to him, chaos about the social fabric of his life. He could not do it. Then with a long breath he set his teeth and opened his lips to denounce her as crazy, but in that instant his eyes fell on her drawn face, and quivering lips. In another moment he saw his conduct of the past years in all its hideousness. Suddenly Judge Brown spoke.

"Mark, what is this? Have you nothing to say?"

He would not glance at Katherine. One look at her fair face would unman him. He turned slowly and faced Judge Brown and there was defiance in his look. All that was noble in his nature spoke at last.

Another instant his arms were about his fond old mother, while she sobbed her heart out on his breast.

Thou Shalt Be

❧

J. B. HOWARD

J. B. Howard

"Thou Shalt Be" was published in the *Indianapolis Freeman* in March 1903, but little is known about the author. The story opens on Christmas morning in Chicago at the turn of the century. The central character, Kirk Rochelle, a young black songwriter, falls asleep while waiting for his friend, Paul Stanley, to arrive for a holiday visit. In the ensuing dream, as Kirk and Paul attend a Christmas matinee show at the famous Alhambra Theatre, where many noted African-American entertainers performed, the author suggests that Christmas is a time for reflecting on one's past and future.

J. B. Howard uses this dream sequence as a segue into African-American history and "Thou Shalt Be" becomes a historical commentary on black life and culture during the late nineteenth and early twentieth centuries. He notes the significance of the Grand United Order of True Reformers, a fraternal organization that served as an insurance company, banking entity, and sponsor of theaters and other businesses. Institutions such as the True Reformers and the Alhambra Theatre were indispensable to the progress of African-Americans in the late nineteenth century. In addition to being models of black success, they provided job opportunities and economic support for fledgling black enterprises.

Howard's recognition of black performers, such as Billy McClain, Ernest Hogan, Sissieretta Jones, Billy Kersands, Bob Cole, and others who were the "headliners" of their day, and the pioneers who opened doors previously closed to African-Americans, reminded the readers of their history and their struggle, as a black people, to advance in the United States.

This story is a social commentary on a number of issues that engaged black Americans in the late nineteenth century. Howard's assertions about Booker T. Washington, "the great educator and Moses of our people," and especially his declaration that since Washington's day "have come greater men than he," is a political statement about black leadership.

Focusing on the experiences of Paul Stanley, Howard also interjects information about the administration of President William McKinley, and the important impact of the Spanish-American War on black employment in government teaching positions in Puerto Rico. Although white female teachers were initially employed following the end of the war and U.S. occupation of the island, it became more feasible to hire African-Americans to work with the largely mixed-race Puerto Rican population.

These are only a few of the many allusions Howard makes to the history of African-Americans. "Thou Shalt Be" reinforces the belief that in the thirty-eight years following Emancipation black people had made significant progress. He suggests that they had a great deal to be thankful for, and much to look forward to, and what better time to give thanks and celebrate than at Christmas.

Thou Shalt Be

∾

Kirk Rochelle was nothing if not a day dreamer. His quixotic fancy and powers of [imagination] always pandered to the seemingly impossible, and yet at the same time, most of the phantoms his [truant] thoughts were pleased to chase were invariably clothed with a plausibility which would [astound] his friends when he chose to expound them. On the particular day this little tale opens, which by the way was Christmas morning, our philosophic theorist was quietly seated by his little desk in a modest, but neatly furnished apartment of his quiet home, abstractedly gazing into the smoldering embers of the well-filled fireplace. Kirk had been unusually successful and was rapidly gaining a national reputation as a rising young colored song writer. Some of the best publishing houses had put out his [music], and the Negro theatrical profession had swarmed to him as the coming genius of his race in supplying them with tuneful lyrics.

Something had evidently gone amiss with him on this particular morning. The truth was he had been sorely put out by the failure of an old school chum to put in an appearance. Paul Stanley had written him more than three weeks before that he would surely be in Chicago and would spend the holidays as his guest. Christmas day had come and was fast passing away yet no Paul.

"Confound it, why could he not have had the good grace to write a fellow a line and explain if he were not coming. However, I shan't be too hard in my criticism just yet, as I strongly suspect his fellow-townsmen have extended him such a cordial welcome on his return to the states from his long labors in the Islands that he has been too upset to even think of me or his engagement. Then, too, he may have put off his coming to the last moment in order to give me a genuine Christmas surprise. I shall wait till noon before I give [up on] him."

Kirk stretched himself out in his chair as he finished this little soliloquy and running his hands into his trousers pockets, leaned his head lazily back into the big armed chair. He was seated thus for some moments still gazing into the fire, when lo he looked up and there stood his friend Paul Stanley—big, robust, healthy Paul of old. He thought his friend looked quite stunning in his English cut raiment, which set his tanned complexion off to a nicety that was really attractive.

"Well, by all that is holy," exclaimed Kirk, springing from his seat and grasping the proffered hand of his friend, "if it isn't you Paul, old man, at last! Really I had about given you [up], and was beginning to think how I was going to offer an excuse to my friends up at the club, where I have arranged a little spread for 5 o'clock this afternoon in your honor."

"It was an unavoidable detention I assure you, old fellow," quickly apologized Paul. "That beastly train had to be more than three hours late. However, I am here and yours—all yours for the rest of the week."

"Do sit down and warm yourself," said Kirk, pushing a chair up to the fire. "Ah, that's better," he went on, [hanging] his friend's raglan over the back of a chair and placing his hat on the desk. "Now old man while I am mixing a toddy, sail right in and tell me something of your educational labors in Puerto Rico, I am dying to know."

"Well, to start with, I like it immensely. The petty prejudices with which I had first to contend consequent upon the spasmodic exodus of Southern white women to the field, shortly after my appointment as you will remember, have, in a measure, all passed away, and I am glad to say that I am getting on swimmingly. In this particular governmental employment Uncle Sam is certainly treating his agents as one and the same. The seeds planted by the McKinley administration immediately after the occupation of the Island at the close of the Spanish-American war, have developed into wholesome results, and the precedents then established have never been altered as regards the survival of the fittest. The white teachers have begun to look upon the field as belonging in [particular] to Negro labor. This is due, old man, to the [mixture] of the people, the result of the Old Spanish regime and its brutal miscegenation. I am now drawing first class pay, having worked myself up, as you know, from an humble assistant. It is a good field for all Negroes, both men and women, who have any knowledge of the Spanish language and are willing to weather the isolation, and can, of course, pass the examination. But more of this anon. Tell me what shall we be doing to while away the time between now and the hour set for your little dinner party?"

As this little recitation was finished relative to his connection with the government in the capacity of teacher to the Puerto Rican children in the faraway Island, Paul arose and accepted the glass which Kirk extended. "Confound you, old man, I am [proud] of you," observed Rochelle as he looked admiringly at his companion. "We will reserve further of this interesting talk 'till we get to the club this evening where I am sure the other fellows will be delighted to listen in rapture to your narrative."

After a short discussion of the dear old school life they had spent together in the sweet long ago, and the thousand and one amusing events incident thereto, the two friends started downtown to take in a Christmas matinee as a means of whiling away the time until dinner, which was ordered at 5 o'clock at the Appomattox Club.

"Time brings many changes, eh, old man?" observed Paul, as they strolled leisurely along.

"I should say it does," responded Kirk. "Let me see, how long has it been since we met? Why, bless me, it must be fully twelve years."

"Quite," answered Paul.

"It seems almost impossible for me to conceive the rapid flight of time. Do you remember, Paul, how about ten years after McKinley's assassination when the dawn of the Negro's new Emancipation from the prejudices of that period were just beginning to bud into tangible existence, our old professor used to preach to us of the new era just opening up to the Negro, and how events were then pointing to indications which bespoke his ultimate salvation from conditions with which we were then environed. Oh how we knowing ones used to laugh and put it all down as so much rot. We then thought that Booker T. Washington—the great educator and Moses of our people—had put forth the only practical solution of the great problem which at that time confronted and agitated the people. But ah, my boy, since his day have come greater men than he, at whom the people now marvel as the concentrators and manipulators of the combined moneyed interests of our race."

"You are right Kirk," said Paul. "Of course you refer to that mighty band, the True Reformers?"

"I do indeed," replied Kirk. "Don't you know at times I can scarcely realize the magnitude of that concern? As I said before, they have proven the greatest concentrating agent of an improvident race's wealth this world will ever know again. Let me see: it was during

Fairbanks' first administration, I think—yes, I am quite sure—for he was the next President after the second term of Roosevelt, was he not?"

Paul nodded a quiet assent.

"Well, it was then," he went on, "that they first attracted the attention of the world as a formidable and rapidly growing factor destined to be one of the great money powers of America: and now we have ample proof of the exactness of that prediction all around us. In every state their amalgamated interests and acquisition of various properties is positively appalling."

"Yes, I think the founders of this institution will ever remain the idols of Negro history," said Stanley. "We are to be thankful that the American people showed their wisdom in sending that gallant man Johnson, of Ohio, to the Presidential seat at the most critical moment in the history of this organization. I mean directly after Fairbanks. They could not have sent a better exponent and advocate of the principles of civic justice to all than he. Don't you remember how the Association of American Bankers about this time had begun to cast suspicious glances at the various banking establishments this organization [was] putting into operation in different sections of the country, and how their mutterings were going abroad to the people in concerted voice relative to the growing substantiality and ambitions of the Negroes along this line? Well, they got no encouragement from

President Johnson, who flatly refused, if you remember, to lend his support to any measure tending to restrict the progress of this work. He pointed out that the fundamental basis upon which his political career had been built, dated from the very day on which he took the stand of the common people's friend in the great street railway upheaval in Cleveland twenty years before. Therefore, he decided that he would assist any movement by which the interests of this corporation might be furthered."

"True, I remember distinctly," said Kirk. "We will never have a greater friend than he proved to be throughout the eight years of his incumbency. Here we are, old fellow, at the Alhambra, one of the leading colored theatres of the city. This is one of the large theatrical properties the True Reformers own and operate throughout the country."

"A magnificent structure truly," exclaimed Paul enthusiastically, "yes this is, I believe, their largest house in the West, yet I am told they control larger ones in New York and Boston."

The building at whose portals they had halted was indeed a magnificent piece of architecture, massive and modern in design. Kirk remarked to his friend that they had lots of time before the curtain rose and suggested that they linger in the lobby and inspect minutely the elegant oil paintings which decorated the walls on either side. They stopped in front of a colossal gothic pillow forming one of the supports in the entrance upon which was an elaborately done portrait in oil.

"Who is this?" asked Paul, pointing to the picture. "His looks of gray give him an exceptionally distinguished bearing."

"Why, that is the famous Dunbar, author, poet and dramatist," answered Kirk.

"Not Paul Laurence?"

"The same. He is styled the 'grand old man of literature.' He is the author of the play we are to see here this afternoon," continued Kirk. "It has had quite a run; this is its fifth week."

"You don't say."

"Yes, and I think it is going to 'go big' (as the professionals would say) over the entire circuit. Its most powerful novelty lies in the fact that it is the first society drama this talented old man has put before the public wherein every character depicted is a Negro, and every scene aflame with the progress and domestic customs of our present people."

The two passed on slowly down the lobby stopping for a brief explanation at each picture.

"Oh!" exclaimed Paul, as they halted in front of a handsomely framed double portrait, "that is the once famous team, Williams & Walker. I remember having read of them quite often in *The Freeman Gazette* — a theatrical journal gotten out weekly by the management of The Freeman Publishing Co., in conjunction with their regular issue of their great paper."

"Yes, they are revered by the entire profession as the first link in the now almost endless chain of theatrical successes and top-notch stars," observed Kirk. "Although the present day and customs have brought unique departures from the creations these great actors and thinkers put forth in their time, yet, through the vista of declining years we look back with much pride upon the hard won success of these men twenty five years ago."

So they passed on and on, up one side and [down] the other, discussing the different actresses and actors who were the big successes of the season. Occasionally they came to some stately photographs of white headed old men who had been pronounced "headliners" in their day. Billy McClain, Ernest Hogan, Billy Kersands, Bob Cole, Irving Jones, Avery & Hart, Sissieretta Jones and many other renowned faces came in for their respective share of comment as to their relative worth and merit in the day and time when they were the representatives of the Negro's theatrical ability before the world. Some little time had been consumed in the inspection of the pictures, and to their surprise, the two young men found the theatre comfortably filled when they entered and were ushered to their seats.

The audience at once attracted attention. (Most holiday matinees do.) The gowns worn by the ladies of the several box assemblies were perfect creations of the modistes latest designs.

"Who is that distinguished looking young chap over there in the lower box with the glasses?", inquired Paul after he and Kirk had settled comfortably in their seats and finished their first hasty scrutiny of the surroundings.

"Oh, that is Clarence Jones," replied Kirk. "He is one, if not the most acceptable party from a financial point of view, in all 'Coon swelldom.' His father made the bulk of his money years ago in the transfer business, and he is estimated variously to be the possessor of from three to five hundred thousand dollars, with a business interest that turns to his account more than thirty thousand dollars a year."

"Gee whiz!" was Paul's reply.

"Pshaw," continued Kirk, "that's nothing; the young lady in pink to his right, Miss B——, a grand-niece or something of the kind to the famous John Johnson, whom you doubtless remember as the great factor who attracted so much attention in the liquor business some twelve or fifteen years ago, is [heiress] to something close to a million in her own name."

Just here the orchestra struck up a catchy air and for the time being the two friends were prevented from further discourse along these lines. In a few moments the curtain arose and they were drifted with profound interest into the story of the play. As it unfolded itself the drama told a beautiful tale; Dunbar had named it: "The Drifting of the Ways." In style of theme and general construction it bore a striking resemblance to David Belasco's powerful drama called "The Lost

Paradise," which had been so favorably received by the people more than thirty-five years before. The characters were all Negroes. The pictures presented the race in all the glory of inventive mechanical and social achievements. The last act was rife with platitudes of the choicest dialogue, and fairly teeming with nicely drawn situations. Paul with his characteristic impetuosity, had lost himself completely in the ideality of the character assumed by the heroine of the play. As the story went, she was the beautiful and accomplished daughter of a Negro manufacturer who had conducted successfully for a number of years a huge implement factory near the vicinity of Birmingham, Alabama. Events proved that his confidential superintendent, who was desperately in love with the girl, had secretly invented a patent which he was pushing quietly, not daring to disclose his affections to the haughty father of the girl. Through all of his embarrassments consequent upon his struggles to keep up appearances in the social set his relations with the girl exacted, she unflinchingly shared them all with him. Her sweet voice and ever present encouragement tided him over many places where, otherwise, the despair and failure which seemed inevitable, would surely have engulfed him.

"By jove!" exclaimed Paul as the curtain lowered on the last scene, "she certainly was a 'sticker' in the artificial; wonder how she is in the real? Surely, old man, you can arrange for me to meet her?"

"Certainly," responded Kirk as they were elbowing their way down the aisle toward the door. The crush was something stifling. All of a sudden the lights were extinguished and the house was in dense darkness. When the light next dawned to the eyes of the befuddled Kirk, he sprang to his feet with a cry of surprise. For lo! he was still in his modest little room at home, the fire had gone out in the grate. With a sense of numb stiffness he realized that it had all been a dream.

General Washington: A Christmas Story

Pauline Elizabeth Hopkins

Pauline Elizabeth Hopkins

Pauline Elizabeth Hopkins, the author of "General Washington: A Christmas Story," also wrote "The Test of Manhood." This story, published in the December 1900 issue of the *Colored American Magazine,* is very rich in black speech, folklore, and culture. It includes a number of themes related to the African-American condition at the turn of the twentieth century. Set in Washington, D.C., Hopkins's story uses social commentary to focus on issues related to racism, religion, the survival of the urban black poor, spousal abuse, child neglect and abuse, crime, and even miscegenation. This is all accomplished through an exploration of the exploits of "General Washington."

The central characters of this story are General Washington, Fairy, and Senator Tallman. General Washington, also known as Buster, is a formally uneducated but street-smart ten-year-old orphan who is hustling for survival among the food and produce stalls at the Washington Market in the District of Columbia where "his specialty was selling chitlins." He is a "knight of the pavement," who dances on the street and in saloons for pay; a leader of a gang of street urchins; a survivor who "lived in the very shady atmosphere of Murderer's Bay" in a box turned on end and filled with straw. Fairy, the granddaughter of Senator Tallman, a United States Senator, meets General Washington while shopping with her nanny. Following a brief observation of General Washington unscrupulously selling chitterlings to buyers in the market, Fairy introduces herself and invites him to come to her home on Christmas morning to learn about God and atone for his un-Christian ways. Senator Tallman himself is a former slave owner and Confederate veteran. He is an embittered man, who professes his hatred for "Negroes" and opposes any black advancement.

Hopkins skillfully uses naming as a device to delineate the characters. Thus, "General," or "Buster," is a leader: "General Washington ranked first among the knights of the pavement." Fairy represents an imaginary, tiny, graceful figure that the General had learned about in his short stay at school. When he meets the blue-eyed, well-dressed, white Fairy, he is awestruck. Hopkins describes Tallman as a larger-than-life, pompous racist, who is preparing to deliver a speech before the Senate that would "bury the blacks too deep for resurrection and settle the Negro question forever." Tallman, the fictional senator, is in some ways a parody of the real life Senator Ben Tillman, who gained great visibility during the 1870s as an activist in the movement to overthrow the Republican-dominated Reconstruction government in South Carolina. A rabid Negro-hater, he was elected governor of South Carolina in 1890, and by 1894 was in the U.S. Senate. Tillman was widely known for his virulent racist comments and conscientious efforts to pass the South Carolina Constitution of 1895, which disfranchised African-American men. Through the characters of the General and Senator Tallman, Hopkins demonstrates that Christmas is a time of rebirth, salvation, and redemption in Christ.

Hopkins refers to a particular cultural practice that is not well known today: the Juba, a popular slave dance based on an African step called Giouba, an elaborate jig. Like his forebears, General Washington and other dancers engaged in competitions to determine who was the most skillful and agile dancer, and who could dance the best and the longest.

General Washington: A Christmas Story

༃

I

General Washington did any odd jobs he could find around the Washington market, but his specialty was selling chitlins.

General Washington lived in the very shady atmosphere of Murderer's Bay in the capital city. All that he could remember of [his] father or mother in his ten years of miserable babyhood was that they were frequently absent from the little shanty where they were supposed to live, generally after a protracted spell of drunkenness and bloody quarrels when the police were forced to interfere for the peace of the community. During these absences, the child would drift from one squalid home to another wherever a woman—God save the mark!—would take pity upon the poor waif and throw him a few scraps of food for his starved stomach, or a rag of a shawl, apron or skirt, in winter, to wrap about his attenuated little body.

One night the General's daddy being on a short vacation in the city, came home to supper; and because there was no supper to eat, he occupied himself in beating his wife. After that time, when the officers took him, the General's daddy never returned to his home. The General's mammy? Oh, she died!

General Washington's resources developed rapidly after this. Said resources consisted of a pair of nimble feet for dancing the hoedown, shuffles intricate and dazzling, and the Juba; a strong pair of lungs, a wardrobe limited to a pair of pants originally made for a man, and tied about the ankles with strings, a shirt with one gallows, a vast amount of "brass," and a very, very small amount of nickel. His education was practical; "Ef a corn-dodger costs two cents, an' a fellar hain't got de two cents, how's he gwine ter git de corn-dodger?"

General Washington ranked first among the knights of the pavement. He could shout louder and hit harder than any among them; that was the reason they called him "Buster" and "the General." The General could swear, too; I am sorry to admit it, but the truth must be told.

He uttered an oath when he caught a crowd of small white aristocrats tormenting a kitten. The General landed among them in quick time and commenced knocking heads at a lively rate. Presently he was master of the situation, and marched away triumphantly with the kitten in his arms, followed by stones and other missiles which whirled about him through space from behind the safe shelter of back yards and street corners.

The General took the kitten home. Home was a dry-goods box

turned on end and filled with straw for winter. The General was as happy as a lord in summer, but the winter was a trial. The last winter had been a hard one, and Buster called a meeting of the leading members of the gang to consider the advisability of moving farther south for the hard weather.

"'Pears lak to me, fellers, Wash'nton's heap colder'n it uster be, an' I'se mighty onscruplus 'bout stoppin' hyar."

"Business am mighty peart," said Teenie, the smallest member of the gang, "s'pose we put off menderin' tell after Chris'mas; Jeemes Henry, fellers, it hain't no Chris'mas fer me outside ob Wash'nton."

"Dat's so, Teenie," came from various members as they sat on the curbing playing an interesting game of craps.

"Den hyar we is tell after Chris'mas, fellers; then dis sonny's gwine ter move, sho, hyar me?"

"De gang's wid yer, Buster; move it is."

It was about a week before Chris'mas, and the weather had been unusually severe.

Probably because misery loves company—nothing could be more miserable than his cat—Buster grew very fond of Tommy. He would cuddle him in his arms every night and listen to his soft purring while he confided all his own hopes and fears to the willing ears of his four-footed companion, occasionally pulling his ribs if he showed any signs of sleepiness.

But one night poor Tommy froze to death. Buster didn't—more's the wonder—only his ears and his two big toes. Poor Tommy was thrown off the dock into the Potomac the next morning, while a stream of salt water trickled down his master's dirty face, making visible, for the first time in a year, the yellow hue of his complexion. After that the General hated all flesh and grew morose and cynical.

Just about a week before Tommy's death, Buster met the fairy. Once, before his mammy died, in a spasm of reform she had forced him to go to school, against his better judgment, promising the teacher to go up and "wallop" the General every day if he thought Buster needed it. This gracious offer was declined with thanks. At the end of the week the General left school for his own good and the good of the school. But in that week he learned something about fairies; and so, after she threw him the pinks that she carried in her hand, he called her to himself "the fairy."

Being Christmas week, the General was pretty busy. It was a great sight to see the crowds of people coming and going all day long about the busy market; wagon loads of men, women and children, some carts drawn by horses, but more by mules. Some of the people well-dressed, some scantily clad, but all intent on getting enjoyment out of this their leisure season. This was the season for selling crops and settling the year's account. The store-keepers, too, had prepared their most tempting wares, and the thoroughfares were crowded.

"I 'clare to de Lord, I'se done busted my ol' man, shure," said one woman to another as they paused to exchange greetings outside a store door.

"N'em min'," returned the other, "he'll wurk fer mo'. Dis is Chris'mas, honey."

"To be sure," answered the first speaker, with a flounce of her ample skirts.

Meanwhile her husband pondered the advisability of purchasing [a] mule, feeling in his pockets for the price demanded, but finding them nearly empty. The money had been spent on the annual festival.

"Ole mule, I want yer mighty bad, but you'll have to slide dis time; it's Chris'mas, mule."

The wise old mule actually seemed to laugh as he whisked his tail against his bony sides and steadied himself on his three sound legs.

The vendors were very busy, and their cries were wonderful for ingenuity of invention to attract trade:

"Hellow, dar, in de cellar, I'se got fresh aggs fer de'casion; now's yer time fer agg-nogg wid new aggs in it."

There were the stalls, too, kept by venerable aunties and filled with specimens of old-time southern cheer: Coon, corn-pone, possum fat and hominy; there were piles of gingerbread and boiled chestnuts, heaps of walnuts and roasting apples. There were great barrels of cider, not to speak of something stronger. There were terrapin and the persimmon [seed] and the chinquapin [nut] in close proximity to the succulent viands—shine and spare-rib, sausage and crackling, savory souvenirs of the fine art of hog-killing. And everywhere were faces of dusky hue; Washington's great Negro population bubbled over in every direction.

The General was peddling chitlins. He had a tub upon his head and was singing in his strong childish tones:

> *"Here's yer chitlins, fresh an' sweet.*
> *Young hog's chitlins hard to beat,*
> *Methodis chitlins, jes' been biled,*
> *Right fresh chitlins, dey ain't spiled,*
> *Baptis' chitlins by de pound,*
> *As nice chitlins as ever was foun."*

"Hyar, boy, duz yer mean ter say dey is real Baptis' chitlins, sho nuff?"

"Yas, mum."

"How duz you make dat out?"

"De hog raised by Mr. Robberson, a hard-shell Baptis', mum."

"Well, lem-me have two poun's."

"Now," said a solid-looking man as General finished waiting on a crowd of women and men, "I want some o' de Methodes chitlins you's bin hollerin' 'bout."

"Hyar dey is, ser."

"Take 'em all out o' same tub?"

"Yas, ser. Only dair leetle mo' water on de Baptis' chitlins, an' dey's whiter."

"How you tell 'em?"

"Well, ser, two hog's chitlins in dis tub an one ob de hogs raised by Unc' Bemis, an' he's a Methodes', ef dat don't make him a Methodes hog nuthin' will."

"Weigh me out four pounds, ser."

In an hour's time the General had sold out. Suddenly at his elbow he heard a voice:

"Boy, I want to talk to you."

The fairy stood beside him. She was a little girl about his own age, well wrapped in costly velvet and furs; her long, fair hair fell about her like an aureole of glory; a pair of gentle blue eyes set in a sweet, serious face glanced at him from beneath a jaunty hat with a long curling white feather that rested light as thistle-down upon the beautiful curly locks. The General could not move for gazing, and as his wonderment grew his mouth was extended in a grin that revealed the pearly whiteness of two rows of ivory.

"Boy, shake hands."

The General did not move; how could he?

"Don't you hear me?" asked the fairy, imperiously.

"Yas'm," replied the General meekly. "'Deed, missy, I'se 'tirely too dirty to tech dem clos o' yourn."

Nevertheless he put forth timidly and slowly a small paw begrimed with the dirt of the street. He looked at the hand and then at her; she looked at the hand and then at him. Then their eyes meeting, they laughed the sweet laugh of the free-masonry of childhood.

"I'll excuse you this time, boy," said the fairy, graciously, "but you must remember that I wish you to wash your face and hands when you are to talk with me; and," she added, as though inspired by an afterthought, "it would be well for you to keep them clean at other times, too."

"Yas'm," replied the General.

"What's your name, boy?"

"Gen'r'l Wash'nton," answered Buster, standing at attention as he had seen the police do in the court-room.

"Well, General, don't you know you've told a story about the chitlins you've just sold?"

"Tol' er story?" queried the General with a knowing look. "Course I got to sell my chitlins ahead ob de oder fellars, or lose my trade."

"Don't you know it's wicked to tell stories?"

"How come so?" asked the General, twisting his bare toes about in his rubbers, and feeling very uncomfortable.

"Because, God says we musn't."

"Who's he?"

The fairy gasped in astonishment. "Don't you know who God is?"

"No'pe; never seed him. Do he live in Wash'nton?"

"Why, God is your Heavenly Father, and Christ was His son. He was born on Christmas Day a long time ago. When He grew [to be a] man, wicked men nailed Him to the cross and killed Him. Then He went to heaven, and we'll all live with Him some day if we are good before we die. O I love Him; and you must love Him, too, General."

"Now look hyar, missy, you kayn't make this chile b'lieve nufin lak dat."

The fairy went a step nearer the boy in her eagerness:

"It's true; just as true as you live."

"Whar'd you say He lived?"

"In heaven," replied the child, softly.

"What kin' o' place is heaven?"

"Oh, beautiful!"

The General stared at the fairy. He worked his toes faster and faster.

"Say, kin yer hab plenty to eat up dar?"

"O, yes; you'll never be hungry there."

"An' a fire, an' clos?" he queried in suppressed, excited tones.

"Yes; it's all love and plenty when we get to heaven, if we are good here."

"Well, missy, dat's a pow'ful good story, but I'm blamed ef I b'lieve it." The General forgot his politeness in his excitement.

"An' ef it's true, tain't only fer white fo'ks; you won't fin' nary nigger dar."

"But you will; and all I've told you is true. Promise me to come to my house on Christmas morning and see my mother. She'll help you, and she will teach you more about God. Will you come?" she asked eagerly, naming a street and number in the most aristocratic quarter of Washington. "Ask for Fairy, that's me. Say quick; here is my nurse."

The General promised.

"Law, Miss Fairy, honey; come right hyar. I'll tell yer mamma how you's done run 'way from me to talk to dis dirty little monkey. Pickin' up sech trash fer ter talk to."

The General stood in a trance of happiness. He did not mind the slurring remarks of the nurse, and refrained from throwing a brick at the buxom lady, which was a sacrifice on his part. All he saw was the glint of golden curls in the winter sunshine, and the tiny hand waving him good-by.

"Ah' her name is Fairy! Jes' ter think how I hit it all by my lone-some."

Many times that week the General thought and puzzled over Fairy's words. Then he would sigh:

"Heaven's where God lives. Plenty to eat, warm fire all de time in winter; plenty o' clos', too, but I'se got to be good. 'Spose dat means keepin' my face an' hand's clean an' stop swearing' an' lyin'. It kayn't be did."

The gang wondered what had come over Buster.

II

The day before Christmas dawned clear and cold. There was snow on the ground. Trade was good, and the General, mindful of the visit next day, had bought a pair of second-hand shoes and a new calico shirt.

"Git onter de dude!" sang one of the gang as he emerged from the privacy of the dry-goods box early Christmas Eve.

The General was a dancer and no mistake. Down at Dutch Dan's place they kept the old-time Southern Christmas moving along in hot time until the dawn of Christmas Day stole softly through the murky atmosphere. Dutch Dan's was the meeting place of the worst characters, white and black, in the capital city. From that vile den issued the twin spirits murder and rapine as the early winter shadows fell; there the criminal entered in the early dawn and was lost to the accusing eye of justice. There was a dance at Dutch Dan's Christmas Eve, and the General was sent for to help amuse the company.

The shed-like room was lighted by oil lamps and flaring pine torches. The center of the apartment was reserved for dancing. At one end the inevitable bar stretched its yawning mouth like a monster awaiting his victims. A long wooden table was built against one side of the room, where the game could be played to suit the taste of the most expert devotee of the fickle goddess.

The room was well filled, early as it was, and the General's entrance was the signal for a shout of welcome. Old Unc' Jasper was tuning his fiddle and blind Remus was drawing sweet chords from an old banjo. They glided softly into the music of the Mobile shuffle. The General began to dance. He was master of the accomplishment. The pigeon-wing, the old buck, the hoe-down and the Juba followed each other in rapid succession. The crowd shouted and cheered and joined in the sport. There was hand-clapping and a rhythmic accompaniment of patting the knees and stamping the feet. The General danced faster and faster:

> *"Juba up and juba down,*
> *Juba all aroun' de town;*
> *Can't you hyar de juba pat? Juba!"*

sang the crowd. The General gave fresh graces and new embellishments. Occasionally he added to the interest by yelling, "Ain't dis fin'e!" "Oh, my!" "Now I'm gittin' loose!" "Hol' me, hol' me!"

The crowd went wild with delight.

The child danced until he fell exhausted to the floor. Someone in the crowd "passed the hat." When all had been waited upon the bar-keeper counted up the receipts and divided fair — half to the house and half to the dancer. The fun went on, and the room grew more crowded. General Wash'nton crept under the table and curled himself up like a ball. He was lucky, he told himself sleepily, to have so warm a berth that cold night; and then his heart glowed as he thought of the morrow and Fairy, and wondered if what she had said were true. Heaven must be a fine place if it could beat the floor under the table for comfort and warmth. He slept. The fiddle creaked, the dancers shuffled. Rum went down their throats and wits were befogged. Suddenly the General was wide awake with a start. What was that?

"The family are all away to-night at a dance, and the servants gone home. There's no one there but an old man and a kid. We can be well out of the way before the alarm is given. 'Leven sharp, Doc. And, look here, what's the number agin?"

Buster knew in a moment that mischief was brewing, and he turned over softly on his side, listening mechanically to catch the reply. It came. Buster sat up. He was wide awake then. They had given the street and number where Fairy's home was situated.

III

Senator Tallman was from Maryland. He had owned slaves, fought in the Civil War on the Confederate side, and at its end had been returned to a seat in Congress after Reconstruction, with feelings of deeply rooted hatred for the Negro. He openly declared his purpose to oppose their progress in every possible way. His favorite argument was disbelief in God's handiwork as shown in the Negro.

"You argue, suh, that God made 'em, I have my doubts, suh, God made man in His own image, suh, and that being the case, suh, it is clear that he had no hand in creating niggers. A nigger, suh, is the image of nothing but the devil." He also declared in his imperious, haughty, Southern way; "The South is in the saddle, suh, and she will never submit to the degradation of Negro domination; never suh."

The Senator was a picture of honored age and solid comfort seated in his velvet armchair before the fire of blazing logs in his warm, well-lighted study. His lounging coat was thrown open, revealing its soft silken lining, his feet were thrust into gayly embroidered fur-lined slippers. Upon the baize covered table beside him a silver salver sat holding a decanter, glasses and fragrant mint, for the Senator loved the beguiling sweetness of a mint julep at bedtime. He was writing a speech which in his opinion would bury the blacks too deep for resurrection and settle the Negro question forever. Just now he was idle; the evening paper was folded across his knees; a smile was on his face. He was alone in the grand mansion, for the festivities of the season had begun and the family were gone to enjoy a merry-making at the house of a friend. There was a picture in his mind of Christmas in his old Maryland home in the good old days "befo' de wah," the great ballroom where giggling girls and matrons fair glided in the stately minuet. It was in such a gathering he had met his wife, the beautiful Kate Channing. Ah, the happy time of youth and love! The house was very still; how loud the ticking of the clock sounded. Just then a voice spoke beside his chair:

"Please, sah, I'se Gen'r'l Wash'nton."

The Senator bounded to his feet with an exclamation:

"Eh! Bless my soul, suh; where did you come from?"

"Ef yer please, boss, froo de winder."

The Senator rubbed his eyes and stared hard at the extraordinary figure before him. The Gen'r'l closed the window and then walked up to the fire, warmed himself in front, then turned around and stood with his legs wide apart and his shrewd little gray eyes fixed upon the man before him.

The Senator was speechless for a moment; then he advanced upon the intruder with a roar warranted to make a six-foot man quake in his boots:

"Through the window, you black rascal! Well, I reckon you'll go out through the door, and that in quick time, you little thief."

"Please, boss, it hain't me; it's Jim the crook and de gang from Dutch Dan's."

"Eh!" said the Senator again.

"What's yer cronumter say now, boss? 'Leven is de time fer de perfahmance ter begin. I reckon'd I'd git hyar time nuff fer yer ter call de perlice."

"Boy, do you mean for me to understand that burglars are about to raid my house?" demanded the Senator, a light beginning to dawn upon him.

The General nodded his head:

"Dat's it, boss, ef by 'buglers' you mean Jim de crook and Dutch Dan." It was ten minutes of the hour by the Senator's watch. He went to the telephone, rang up the captain of the nearest station, and told him the situation. He took a revolver from a drawer of his desk and advanced toward the waiting figure before the fire.

"Come with me. Keep right straight ahead through that door; if you attempt to run I'll shoot you."

They walked through the silent house to the great entrance doors and there awaited the coming of the police. Silently the officers surrounded the house. Silently they crept up the stairs into the now darkened study. "Eleven" chimed the little silver clock on the mantel. There was the stealthy tread of feet a moment after, whispers, the flash of a dark lantern, — a rush by the officers and a stream of electricity flooded the room.

"It's the nigger did it!" shouted Jim the crook, followed instantly by the sharp crack of a revolver. General Washington felt a burning pain shoot through his breast as he fell unconscious to the floor. It was all over in a moment. The officers congratulated themselves on the capture they had made — a brace of daring criminals badly wanted by the courts.

When the General regained consciousness, he lay upon a soft, white bed in Senator Tallman's house. Christmas morning had dawned clear cold and sparkling; upon the air the joy-bells sounded sweet and strong: "Rejoice, your Lord is born." Faintly from the streets came the sound of merry voices: "Chris'mas gift, Chris'mas gift."

The child's eyes wandered aimlessly about the unfamiliar room as if seeking and questioning. They passed the Senator and Fairy, who sat beside him and rested on a copy of Titian's matchless Christ which hung over the mantel. A glorious stream of yellow sunshine fell upon the thorn-crowned Christ.

> *"God of Nazareth, see!*
> *Before a trembling soul*
> *Unfoldeth like a scroll*
> *Thy wondrous destiny!"*

The General struggled to a sitting position with arms outstretched, then fell back with a joyous, awesome cry:

"It's Him! It's Him!"

"O' General," sobbed Fairy, "don't you die, you're going to be happy all the rest of your life Grandpa says so."

"I was in time, little Missy; I tried mighty hard after I knowed whar' dem debbils was a-comin' to."

Fairy sobbed; the Senator wiped his eyeglasses and coughed. The General lay quite still a moment, then turned himself again on his pillow to gaze at the pictured Christ.

"I'm a-gittin' sleepy, missy, it's so warm an' comfurtable here. 'Pears lak I feel right happy sence Ise seed Him." The morning light grew brighter. The face of the Messiah looked down as it must have looked when He was transfigured on Tabor's heights. The ugly face of the child wore a strange, sweet beauty. The Senator bent over the quiet figure with a gesture of surprise.

The General had obeyed the call of One whom the winds and waves of stormy human life obey. Buster's Christmas Day was spent in heaven.

For some reason, Senator Tallman never made his great speech against the Negro.

Three Christmas Eves

☙

AUGUSTUS M. HODGES

Augustus M. Hodges

Although Augustus M. Hodges was one of the most prolific writers of his time, his extraordinary record of publication is unrecognized today. The writings of only a few black male authors who published at the turn of the century, for example, Paul Laurence Dunbar, Charles W. Chestnutt, and Sutton Griggs, have been acknowledged. Hodges's numerous essays, feature articles, and short stories remain uncollected. In part, writers like Hodges have received less attention because of where their works appeared. Black writers whose works were published in white periodicals, such as *Harper's Magazine, Century Magazine, Atlantic Monthly, Literary Digest, Critic,* and *Lippincott's Monthly Magazine,* received greater attention. But black journals offered black writers an opportunity to develop commentary about issues of importance to the African-American community that were ignored by white publications.

Hodges, the author of "The Blue and the Gray," which is in

this collection of short stories, also wrote "The Prodigal Daughter" and several other Christmas stories and poems. His fiction reflects a certain ambivalence toward his female characters, in that he interjects comments and develops narrative strategies that depict women, particularly young girls on the brink of womanhood, as naive and in need of protection. Most of his fiction is representative of the late-nineteenth- and early-twentieth-century writings of many black and white writers. At this time, there was a great deal of national focus on the lure and vice of the city and its power to corrupt the morals of young girls and women. Within this context, young women were warned to avoid men who dazzled them with promises of fame and wealth, predators who would seduce and bring them down. Images of good girls who had become fallen women proliferated in late-nineteenth- and early-twentieth-century literature. For Hodges, this was a very personal issue, since his own daughter Sarah was a "fallen" woman and the model for "The Prodigal Daughter," a Christmas story he wrote in 1904.

The plot of this story unfolds on three Christmas Eves. Although Hodges's intent is to warn young women and their parents of the pitfalls of the city, his female characters in this story and in "The Prodigal Daughter" are generally weak and susceptible to exploitation. They lack the independence and power of the females that appear in Frederick Burch's "For Love of Him," Margaret Black's "The Woman," and Eva S. Purdy's "How I Won My Husband," and in the fiction of his well-known female literary counterparts, such as Frances Ellen Watkins Harper and Pauline Hopkins. Instead, Hodges's female characters tend to be the victims of patriarchal values and practices.

"Three Christmas Eves," published in the *Christian Recorder* in December 1903, describes the changes that occur in Emma Capps's life over a period of seventeen years, including events that lead to her precipitous decline, which inevitably takes place on Christmas Eve.

In this morality tale, what happens on the third Christmas Eve (1901) is meant to be a warning to young and naive women unaware of the temptations and dangers of life in the big city.

Three Christmas Eves

ॐ

Chapter I
-EMMA, THE GIRL-

"'Twas the night before Christmas," in H— —, Ky., a thrifty Southern town, with a large colored population, in 1884, that little ten-year-old Emma Capps sat in the rear doorway of her father's neat little cottage, picking a turkey for the Christmas feast. Little Emma was very happy, because, besides the old-fashioned Kentucky Christmas dinner, there was to be at night a birthday party, with music and dancing, as that Christmas was her tenth birthday. A distinguished Negro educator and philanthropist (now dead) used to say that people classed by the white Americans as colored had ten times the shades of the rainbow. Little Emma was one of the tints of that rainbow. She was light brown in complexion, with bright brown eyes and straight black Indian-like hair, and a mouth full of pearls. Her father was the leading carpenter and builder of the town, and "they say" that he was worth $10,000 and the second richest man in H— —. Her mother, besides being a thrifty little housewife, had learned from her father, who was, in his time, a great herb and root doctor, the art of making several salves and herb teas, the healing power of which had more than a local fame.

Their little daughter was their only child, their joy and their hope; and they did everything in their power to have her grow up a refined, educated, useful young woman.

The Christmas dinner—a family reunion—was over; the shades of night covered the town, and a merry lot of little folk enjoyed the birthday party until called for, by their parents at gray dawn. One of the last to leave little Emma's birthday party was a boy two years her senior, in the person of Charles Sumner Brown. "Summie," as he was called (as the town was full of Charleses and Charlies), had been a playmate of Emma's since infancy. Had they been five years older we would call them lovers—"Paul and Virginia," in light brown and black. At last his mother took him home, and the party, like the bright Christmas day, was a thing of the past.

Five years passed, during which time both, as classmates, graduated from the village colored high school as first and second in their class. They were young lovers now—she a refined young lady, he an ambitious youth. He went to New York to seek fame and fortune after the usual romantic parting of lovers to be found only in song and story.

Chapter II
-EMMA, THE MAIDEN-

Emma Capps received for several months three letters a week from her devoted sweetheart and prospective husband, and then she received two, then one, and then—none, for months. Still, like all leading females in song or story (but not in real life), she was true to him.

She was an industrious, refined, simple country maid, happy and content with her lot, since she had schooled herself to forget Charles Sumner Brown, and think of him in only two lights, that he was either dead or untrue—in either case, he was dead to her.

Charles Sumner Brown, when he got to New York City, found out that, from a black man's viewpoint, it was not as bright as it was painted, but still a thousand times brighter to the progressive Negro youth than the so-called "New South." He learned the barber trade, opened a swell barber shop, with three workmen, made lots of money, became a sport, "played the ponies," drove fast horses, and was devoted to women and wine.

Chapter III
-EMMA, THE WOMAN-

"'Twas the night before Christmas," 1896, that Charles Sumner Brown "startled the villagers with strange alarm" when he got off the train at

H — —, Ky., with a carload of trunks. He was dressed in the latest New York style, wore eyeglasses and a gold watch. He hired a "hack" and was driven to the only colored boarding house in town, which bore the name of the Lincoln Hotel. In an hour or so it was known all over town that Charles Sumner Brown had returned to his birthplace, and hundreds of his old friends called to see him. Dressed in his Sunday best, he called upon Emma, who received him politely, but coldly. He gave as his reason for not writing "a press of business." He spent the evening with her, and when church bells and guns announced the birth of Christmas he held her hand as of yore; he told her that he had the same love for her as during his [youth]; he asked her to be his wife, and, if needed, fly with him to New York City. Emma was only a woman, and we will say between the lines that women are strong when they should be weak, and weak when they should be strong. Charles Sumner Brown had no love for the sweet-heart of his youth, but—he had a lust for her innocent beauty and knew that honorable (or seemingly honorable) marriage was the only outlet for his passion.

He proposed immediate marriage, and she accepted, without the knowledge of her parents, and was driven to the house of a strange man, who married them. When she told her father of the steps she had taken, the old man, who had long since lost all confidence in Brown, told her that she had made her bed and must sleep in it. A few days after New Year's, Brown returned to New York City with his wife, and boarded her in a fashionable boarding house on West Fifty-third street. He told her that his business was "downtown," but did not tell her where or what. He spent most of his idle time in her company for the first six months, even going so far as to take her to Brooklyn churches several times. Then his supposed love grew cold, and some weeks she saw nothing of him. As he always told her he was "out of town on business," she believed him, but the boarding house mistress, who was an old lady of experience, did not. She made a startling discovery on one of her detective trips—that Brown had been married before; that his wife left him for just reasons; that he kept two establishments (or homes); that his "place of business" was not down-town, but up-town in the section known as "High Bridge," among the Negro population on West 134th Street; that his "business" consisted of a swell barber parlor, a gambling room in the rear and a "ladies' boarding house" upon three upper floors. She conveyed all this information to Emma, who in company with Mrs. Brink (the boarding house keeper), started out to verify the report. She found out that all, and far more, that Mrs. Brink had told her was the truth. When she met Charles Sumner Brown, she told him all she knew. He laughed at her and told her that she had "better leave well enough alone," as their marriage was a "fake" one, as the man who "married" them was not a minister, but a chum of his, brought from New York for the occasion.

At this information Emma went into hysterics and threw a bay rum bottle at him, which struck him in the forehead, cutting it open. He rushed from the house, not that he was not coward enough to knock her down and beat her lifeless, but that he was too much of a coward to face Mrs. Brink.

Emma for months took care of herself by working in a tailor shop, in which she was the only colored woman. Then the work got dull and she was "laid off;" then Mrs. Brink broke up and went to Philadelphia, and—then Emma saw the wolf at her door, and—then she fell.

Chapter IV
-EMMA, THE UNFORTUNATE-

"'Twas the night before Christmas," 1901, that a group of women of the street, of the lowest class, were in the back room of a low saloon in Bleecker street, New York City. The night was damp and cold, the hour was late. One of those waves of reform that now and then sweep over the great city had washed it clean. Women of the street had been driven from their homes; the better class had located in flats occupied by respectable people; the lower class slept in hallways. Emma, at this time, was a member of the lower class of women of the street.

"Come, girls, youse must git out; it's time ter close up," said the bartender at ten o'clock, and the poor wretches were driven out in the cold.

Emma, the unfortunate, had lost everything—lost her beauty, lost her pride, lost her honor, lost her health, lost—yes—even her hope for a better hereafter. She plod the streets of the great city as in a sad dream. To ask aid from a man might lead to arrest and six months on Blackwell's Island; to ask alms of a woman would be a silent look of contempt.

"I'll ask this colored man coming up the street; he is apt to have more feeling for a poor devil, if not more money than a white man."

The man met her. "Merry Christmas to you, sir. I hope you will have a good time to-morrow. Please give me a quarter to get a night's lodging?"

Without looking into her face, the man put his hand into his pocket and pulled out a half dollar. As he handed it to her their eyes met.

"Heavens! As I live, it's Emma Capps! Why, Emma, what brought you down to this condition?" He was Charles Sykes, an old lover she had jilted in the long, long ago.

"The old, old story," she replied; "a trusting woman, a false man, the wolf at the door and the temptations of a great city—that's all." She said no more, but took the half dollar, went to the nearest restaurant, where she had a beef stew, her first meal in twenty-four hours.

She was herself again. Stirred to life, she reviewed her life on the eve of her birthday. "Too late to reform," she said. "In a few hours it will be my birthday. I will end my life on the day it begins." She tried at several drug stores to get "Rough on Rats" and other poisons. Her face told the druggists at once to what use she was going to put them, and all refused to sell her any poison.

"I have it," she said to herself. "I'll get drunk with the quarter I have, but save three cents for boat fare and jump in the river."

The bells of Greater New York were ringing in Christmas morn; the streets were full of merry young folks blowing "fish horns," when a woman hurried down to the Jersey City ferry, paid her last three cents and got on the boat. When the boat was mid-stream she jumped overboard.

The body of Emma Capps was identified by Charles Sykes, Christmas noon, at the morgue. He had it taken to her native Kentucky village, where it sleeps the sleep of rest. The gossips and sensational papers had lots to say about her. Let us reflect: She was more sinned against than sinning; then, she was in New York City. There is but one great city in the United States for weal or woe, good or bad (the bad in the lead), and that is Greater New York City.

For Love of Him:
A Christmas Story

❧

FREDERICK W. BURCH

Frederick W. Burch

"For Love of Him" was published in the *Indianapolis Freeman* in December 1889 by Frederick W. Burch, an unknown author. Similar to Eva Purdy's "How I Won My Husband," this story suggests that Christmas has the power to cast a magical spell over people, and that the holiday reinforces the power of love. It bolsters the theme that Christmas is a time for loving, sharing, and reuniting with friends and family.

The story centers on John A. Wilson, the only "Afro-American" in the graduating class of an integrated high school, and Katherine Brown, his fiancée. John, who is at least three years older than any of the other graduates, is determined to graduate and to become a minister, but his plans are delayed by the death of his father and his mother's illness. Only with financial support from the community and hard work is John able to achieve his goal. Toward the end of his struggle to acquire a high school education, he becomes engaged to Katherine, an ambitious young woman who rejects his marriage proposal upon learning of his plans to enter the ministry.

Burch skillfully uses the Christmas theme to explore the issue of gender relationships between black men and women. During most of the nineteenth and twentieth centuries, the ministry was one of a few arenas of professional employment available to ambitious young black men. Ministers, along with teachers, formed a part of the core leadership in the black community and were highly respected. Because of the expectations and societal demands placed on a minister, it was criti for a man to marry a woman who understood and was willing to fill the demanding position of a minister's wife. Katherine Brown, an educated, ambitious black woman, was unwilling to marry a poor struggling minister and to play the role of his uncomplaining companion.

Burch also raises significant questions about the power and meaning of love as it relates to gender definitions and relationships. He is particularly concerned about the way in which ambitious educated young black women define their role as women. Burch explores a variety of the significant themes of the time, including ideological issues related to definitions of true womanhood and manhood, racial loyalty, and black middle-class beliefs and aspirations. Written less than twenty years after slavery was abolished, "For Love of Him" also emphasizes the importance of Northern blacks, who have had the benefit of formal education, going to the South to teach and encourage formerly enslaved African-Americans.

Burch raises the question of what is truly important: love or ambition? He emphasizes that Christmas is about forgiveness and the sharing of ourselves and our love with others.

For Love of Him: A Christmas Story

~

It was Commencement night at the High School. Throughout the great assembly room was the rustle of silks and satins; and the delicate odor of perfume mingling with the fragrance of all manner of flowers and plants reached the remotest corner. The elite of the city had gathered this warm June night to see the graduating class bid farewell to its alma mater, and to wish them God-speed on their journey along the path of life—the path which we all tread, and which sooner or later leads to a Life that is more than life or a Death far worse than death. The graduates were doing nobly, and judging from the applause so liberally bestowed, the audience was satisfied to a very high degree.

The [program] had nearly reached its close when expectancy became the order of the night. The class historian, a fair young girl, was delivering that always interesting production, and the next piece on the [program] was an oration: "The Macedonian Cry," by John A. Wilson. Instantly, as the applause bestowed on the fair historian ceased, it broke out afresh for the new speaker, the only Afro-

American in the class, who stood brave and smiling before the audience showing its appreciation of him so finely. It was a proud moment for him truly, for looking backward at the class he could see none of his race, and looking forward over the audience very few; and as he gazed the feeling grew strangely strong; this audience recognized him as a man and looking beyond his color saw the God-given talent which was stamped on every line and feature of his fine intellectual face. Not a handsome face as far as beauty was concerned, but rendered grand and noble by the pure, high-toned thoughts which make any true man's face far more beautiful than the standard set by the world.

As has been said, it was a proud moment for him. Always poor, his whole High School course had been one of toil and hardships for him. But the last year had far surpassed the others in the intensity of its toil and in the trying of his patience, for at the beginning of this last year, which was ending so auspiciously for him, his father had suddenly sickened and died and left him to care for the three brothers and the invalid mother whose very soul was wrapped up in the noble son God had given her, and who now, almost at the beginning of his career, must give up his fair dreams of the future, because she, a poor, sickly woman, must be kept alive at the expense of her son's intellectual life.

He had determined upon entering a Divinity School and fitting himself for a minister of the Gospel, and the thought that she must be the cause of his not following his loved vocation was a terrible one to her. It was more than she could bear to think of, and straightway she declared her intention of working for him so that he would not be compelled to leave his school work. It was then his nobility made itself manifest. Clasping the mother fondly in his arms, he declared his intention of staying in school and supporting her also; and so firmly was his declaration made that the widow concluded to let him follow his own plan, and if she could not help him with her hands, she could at least pray for strength for him.

Then the struggle began. Not to enter his Divinity studies—that must be postponed indefinitely or stopped altogether—but to finish his High School course as a member of the same class in which he had started and to which he had been an ornament so long. It was not long before the report of his toil became noised around the business part of the city and in the school halls. When men told each other how the young man slept but five hours a day regularly and worked all the rest of the time except during his school hours, a movement was set on foot to help him.

Ten months of this struggle had passed. Through the cold of the severe Michigan winter he had steadily persevered, although many a time he thought it would be at the cost of his life. And tonight the reward was his, for he was not only to finish here, but the dream of his life was to be fulfilled, and from here he was to go to the Divinity School, and the mother, whom he loved so dearly, was to be cared for by friends who had been raised up to him in his extreme need. The pride which filled his breast was the pride of a good man, for although he was graduating with scholars who were young in years, he had passed his majority three years ago and all a man's feelings and purposes were his. The pride which filled his breast was different than that which surged through the breasts of his classmates, many of whom came from homes of luxury and the lap of wealth, and to whom work and want were both strangers.

While delivering the thoughts of his fertile, cultivated brain, his eye roamed over the audience and rested more than once on a girl, who for beauty was the equal of any girl in the room. To her two years ago had his heart been given, and all the true, pure love of a life with it. This was before he had determined to become a minister, and many had wondered that this beautiful dashing girl had loved the slow, undemonstrative man, and afterwards she had wondered too, for when a year after their engagement he had announced his determination to become a minister, she, with fine, angry scorn had repulsed him, and had told him in words not to be misunderstood that if he supposed she was going to be a minister's wife, he was mistaken; and that had he declared such to be his intention a year ago, she would be spared the pains of breaking their engagement now. Never would she forget the gentle dignity of his manner on that occasion as, drawing himself up, he said:

"Much as I love you, dear, and much as I would endure for you, I thank God that before it was too late, He has shown me how little true womanhood there is in your nature, and how little fitted you are to become any true man's wife. May God forgive you as I do, and although from this moment you and I go apart, yet should you ever wish to bid me God-speed or to regret the step you have so foolishly taken, do not hesitate."

Tonight, as Katherine Brown sat chained by the matchless stream of eloquence which flowed from his lips, his words came back to her. Did she wish him well? Her heart and lips both answered, yes. Did she regret her step taken? Her heart said once more, what her lips would not say, yes. For time had enlightened her, and the love she had thought to crush would not be crushed, and as she looked at him tonight with new eyes, she saw that instead of a poor, struggling minister, she had lost a rich, triumphant man; rich in Nature's noblest gifts; triumphant in the knowledge that he had conquered and would conquer all obstacles. And as the bursts of applause rang out during and after the oration and as the people crowded 'round him wishing him success and tendering their congratulations to him, the sense of loss came home to her more forcibly than ever. She at least had his permission to wish him well whenever she chose, that was one consolation; and why not do so now? She waited until he was alone and approached him. He was bending over some of his flowers and did not see her or hear her approach.

"You told me once that if ever the chance came or the feeling, to wish you well, I might do so," began she softly, "and now I have come. I congratulate you on the excellence of your oration, and to my congratulations add my heartiest wishes for your welfare."

He listened to the low, calm tones, and then said gently:

"Thank you, Katie." Katie was her old pet name with him. "A word from you does my heart more good than any I have heard to-night. So you have come only to say good luck to me? I thought perhaps, that you had come to tell me I could hope for the future, and at the end of my college life you would be mine."

Her heart rose up in stubborn rebellion to the words she was about to say, but she said them ever so bravely, looking into his eyes bravely and steadily and without flinching:

"Must you continue to think that my old passion lives? It died when our engagement ended, it had been dying before and now it has no place in my thoughts, only as the memory of an unpleasant event I would gladly drive from me. And should I change, suppose I did regret, think you I would tell you? Do you imagine that every instinct of maidenly modesty is so dead within me that I should come to you and beg to be taken back to your love? No! Were you pleading in the dust, if you were dying even, and that word from me would save you, I would see you die ere I spoke it."

"Well," said he painfully and slowly in reply, "I have given you your choice. I may have been mistaken in leaving it all to you to say, but I spoke once, and when speaking is done between us again, you will do it. Good by."

He had gone, leaving her where she stood, a sense of shame and humiliation gradually filling her and crushing her beneath its weight. She, the proud woman, who had seen many men leave her side, and had given them not even as much as a thought, felt humbled to the dust. But her pride came to her aid.

"It is better," she said to herself. "He has gone out of my life, and he shall stay out of it."

She kept her word.

"Katie dear, won't you go out with me tonight? Our new church is to be dedicated, our new choir and organ will be heard for the first time, and above all our new minister is to preach his opening sermon. I want you to go. You have been here two years, and haven't been out at all; certainly you should go out tonight, and it's Christmas Eve, too."

The speaker was Lizzie McLinn, the teacher of music in the College where our friend Katherine Brown held sway as professor of mathematics. More than four years have passed since we saw her last, and yet she is the same haughty, unbending woman. She had been teaching in this College in the South, and had made but few friends, but Lizzie McLinn was her firm friend.

If she ever wondered why Katherine was so cold and reserved, she never gave words to her wonderment, but loved her because she was from the North, and had been her friend when she came here to teach music.

Katherine yawned slightly. Truth to tell, she was lonely and this was Christmas Eve. Why not go out? Before, she had gone home to spend the holidays, but now she was here to see what a Southern Christmas was like. It was so different from her Christmas at home. Here was warmth, there cold and snow; [and around] her heart a cold, dark despair, which only a most powerful will controlled.

Since she and John had parted they had been as the dead, as far as intercourse with each other was concerned. He had finished, she knew, but where he was located she had not the slightest idea. In her attempt to keep him out of her life she was generally successful, but tonight that face haunted her as the ghosts of the dead haunt their old habitations, and she could not shut out the visions from before her. Yes, she would go anywhere, for to sit here alone and think of the Christmas Eve, so many years ago, when her betrothal occurred, was maddening; so she turned to her friend Lizzie.

"Your new minister," she said, scornfully. "I suppose he is some old cast off glossed over and palmed off on this suffering, dying congregation as brand new, or else some one who has been worn partially out elsewhere, and has come here to complete the process. Which is it, Lizzie, my dear?"

"It's neither," was the quick reply. "He is very young yet, although he has been preaching already. He rejected a most tempting offer in the North, so that he might come South, where he recognizes the needs of our people. Our church looks beautiful, and every one is enthusiastic over the arrangement of affairs, because a Christmas dedication and installation is a decided innovation, you know. Will you go, Katie, dear?"

"Yes, I'll go," was the short answer.

When they arrived at the church it was crowded. The new minister was evidently there, judging by the satisfied look on the faces of many of the congregation; but he was behind the altar now and could not be seen. Katherine was indulging in the preliminary glance around the church, which women always take when a deep, rich tone she knew too well arrested her attention and drew her gaze to the pulpit.

There he was. The years had used him well, and his old friend Work had agreed to make no inroads on his health; consequently a nobler-looking man than the Rev. John A. Wilson standing behind any sacred desk would be hard to find in the length and breadth of our land. Filled with the Negro's native gift, eloquence, toned and beautiful by educational finishings, it is small wonder that from the time he commenced his sermon until he closed he had his congregation held spellbound and irresistibly drawn to him by the magnetism of his presence, which to a minister counts so much.

His theme was the old, old message of the angels, "Peace on earth, good will to men." It was handled in a masterly way, and the clearness of his language, the brilliance of his logic and the beauty of his eloquence completely carried his audience by storm, and they could almost imagine they were of the party of awe-struck shepherds who heard from angels' lips so many years ago this grand message.

Katherine sat listening, not to the speaker, but the voices within her. Her heart time and again, during the sermon, accused her of throwing away the most priceless jewel ever bestowed on a woman, of crushing a true, pure lover under foot. Her old objection to the life of a minister's wife had gone long ago for the finer, truer sensibilities of her nature had seen the nobility of such a life. What, then, hindered [her]? Nothing but a pride stronger than life or death, a stubborn, unyielding pride which swallowed up every other feeling. And even if she did wish to have him back, if she could humble herself to tell him she had always and would always love him, had his opinion of her changed? Once he had told her she was unfit to be any man's wife and now the words came back to her, and rankled in her heart like an arrow which could not be taken out, except by the hands which placed it there.

She found herself at last, drawn out of her reverie by his closing words.

"Tomorrow all over our civilized earth our Lord's birth is celebrated. Hundreds of years have passed since the angelic host on Bethlehem's plains gave this message which has gone down through the ages and will continue to do its grand work, until time shall be rolled up as a scroll and eternity take its place. Those words have lost none of their meaning or force; if our Creator declared through these heavenly messengers his good feeling for us, may we not in humble imitation of Him strive to spread peace and good will? And how may we do it? By casting aside all pride and malice, by clothing ourselves with the spirit of universal brotherhood and forgiving and forgetting old grudges and enmities, [we can] resolve that we shall not live in vain, and that our world will be made better because we live in it."

When he finished, her mind was made up. Her love had conquered all, and was madly demanding utterance. As though in a vision, she saw the utter folly of having supposed for a moment that he was dead forever to her. She must go to him now even if he rejected her—even if his love were another's—she must go and tell him that now, if never before, she regretted her rash step, and had cast aside pride and malice, and had and would love him always. Her love had humbled her.

She knew he had not seen her—indeed, she knew he was ignorant as to her dwelling place. So she went outside on the church steps and standing away from the door on the upper step, she waited as she had done once before, until he should be alone. Then, she had wished him God speed; now, she was going to ask for the love she had so unwisely rejected. A feeling not much different than fear came over her, but she was determined now, and she would speak.

He came at last. While the sexton was covering the furniture he came to the door alone, as she wished—and looked up at the stars. Involuntarily the words came to his lips.

"Six years ago tonight we were engaged. If I could see her now, my cup of happiness would be full. I forgive and forget all and ask again, just to see her once."

"Katie!"

"John!"

No false pride now on either side; no wrong or selfish thoughts—only true pure love.

"John," she said softly—oh so softly—"can you forgive me, and love me as you did? I—"

"My darling," he interrupted, "my darling, my life, my love, my all, you have come to me once more to-night. You have come to me as—"

"Your Christmas gift, John," she said gaily.

As he pressed his lips once more, the stars shone down upon them, and the old, old song of the angels—the song of all humanity seemed to float and hover around them, making their new betrothal far holier and happier than the old.

"Peace on earth, good will to man."

The Woman:
A Christmas Story

❧

Margaret Black

Margaret Black

Margaret Black, author of a number of short stories and editor of the "Women's Column," which first appeared in the *Baltimore Afro-American* in 1896 and was resurrected in 1916, wrote several short stories that focused more on women's power than women's oppression. Stories such as "A Christmas Party that Prevented a Split in the Church" (1916) and "The Woman" (1915) demonstrate Black's highly refined feminist viewpoint, which is articulated in the subtle strategies she introduces to explore black women's agency as individuals and within organizations.

In "The Woman," Black presents Darl Carew as a powerful, multifaceted woman who is neither a tragic mulatto nor a jezebel. Published by the *Baltimore Afro-American,* this story, unlike most of those written by and about women, does not present the protagonist as a victim, or as oppressed by male culture. Rather, Black presents a complex black female who breaks the mold of what a woman is and what a woman can be. In this way, the story is before its time. Unlike the typical novel of the early twentieth century, this story presents a female who ends up breaking a man, instead of the reverse.

As a feminist, Black utilized symbolic inversion, a narrative strategy that allowed her to demonstrate the pain inflicted upon women and their families by men who thoughtlessly pursued their lustful goals with other women. In 1915 rarely did one find a discussion in literary text about a middle-class black woman who so brazenly breaks the societal moral codes. While this type of behavior was denounced by religious leaders and often by members of the middle class, it was more associated with women entertainers, particularly blues singers who were viewed as being sexually loose and available. Although these women might earn a lot of money, they were perceived as being working class, and were not acceptable in black middle-class circles.

Although not beautiful, Darl has an illusive, indefinable quality that attracts people to her, especially men who vie for her attention. As a person who has huge needs for money, material possessions, and attention, Darl is impulsive and self-centered, and thinks only of the pleasures life has to offer.

The plot centers around Darl's relationship with two men: Royal Dare, her husband, and Matt Walton, her lover. For both of these men, Darl is an enigma, a woman whom they can never subdue or own, and one they will never really know. For Royal Dare, after years of desertion, hurt, disillusionment, and rejection by Darl, Christmas becomes a time for forgiveness. For Matt Walton, Christmas is a time to seek forgiveness, for although he has won "the woman," he has suffered much at the hands of Darl, and has hurt his wife, the woman who loved him.

The Woman: A Christmas Story

☙

> Oh, the years we waste and tears we waste
> And the work of our head, and hand,
> Belong to the woman who did not know,
> (And now we know she never could know)
> And did not understand.
>
> Rudyard Kipling.

"Should he ever see her again?" that was the thought that tugged at his heart, when he sat that night in the dingy hotel room.

He saw her face and her curly brown hair, as plainly as though she had been seated in the room there with him. She had produced such an effect as no woman has produced on him before; and he let her go without knowing from whence she came.

He sighed and said "I must get to work" but it was easier said than done. He could only see her, looking like a fairy, gliding over the ballroom floor, with a word and a smile for all whom she knew. Such a haunting face once seen is never forgotten; he had forgotten most of his partners in watching her; at least this thought consoles him: "The town is small, and I'll soon find her."

But time passed and yet he did not find his "dream face," as he had commenced to call her. Then suddenly one day she appeared coming out of a store and as he stood gazing after her she looked back and smiled.

Six weeks later the Century Club gave another dance, and he was there early, eagerly scanning each face as they appeared; at last he was rewarded by seeing her enter the room on the arm of her escort, Harry West; he managed to get close to the hostess when she greeted her by name; such a sweet name he thought—odd and elusive—Darl Carew.

By sheer good luck he found a friend who knew her and asked for an introduction; at last they could talk, this girl whom he called his "dream face." Pretty, "no," but there was something that drew him to her in spite of himself.

He danced with her and his happiness was complete.

Royal Dare was a mechanical engineer, who had just been in the small town of Somerville a short three months, and his acquaintance was not extensive.

Darl, the girl he admired, was a Somerville girl, liked by every one who knew her; no one ever spoke ugly of her or to her, in fact [she was] a spoilt girl who knew no will but her own. The men vied with each other in showering her with gifts of all kinds, flowers, the best the hot-house had, Bon-Bons, the very best, all were hers without the asking, anything for a smile and a pleasant word. And yet this girl spent her days behind a counter in a dry-goods store, and was the envy of more than half the society girls in the town.

She was a clerk from choice not from necessity, as she had a pleasant home with parents able to care for her; but she wanted more money than they could give her and loved fine clothes so she chose [to] work. Her money was spent on fine clothes. She spent most of her evenings away from home without once being asked as to where she spent the time or with whom she spent it.

When Matt Walton came home from college, he soon joined the crowd who paid homage to Darl, and became one of her most ardent admirers; but among the many he was the only one her parents disliked and was forbidden the privilege of her home, but little difference did that make; they were together constantly, because Darl was so used to having her own way, she paid little heed to her parents' likes or dislikes; it was always a case of self.

At last it came to be a question among the on-lookers as to which man would win the girl; Matt Walton or Royal Dare; both men's chances seemed about equal, and both were prepared to go any lengths to win her.

They hated each other cordially, and were intensely jealous of each other.

Darl knew her power and played with them as a cat does a mouse. If she went to a dance with Matt, she would appease Royal by attending the theatre or spending the evening with him exclusively.

One day Matt was called away by a telegram to a city out of the state and when he returned three months later, no one could tell him anything of Darl, only that she and Royal had disappeared at the same time.

He made a vow to make her rue the day she played him false, as she had promised to marry him and had vowed "she loved only him." They say time heals all wounds, and everybody thought, two years later, that Matt had forgotten Darl Carew, because he married Mary Hay and settled down to work and their home life seemed happy; he became a prosperous business man, President of the largest bank in town, and his name was mentioned for the next Judge of the county court. Two children, a boy and a girl, blessed their home, and any man should have been proud of the family he had; but when alone there were times when he thought of Darl Carew, and would have sacrificed all for her.

In the meantime while Matt was away on business that fateful three months, Royal took advantage of Matt's absence and persuaded Darl to elope with him.

They disappeared as effectually as tho the earth had swallowed them up. No one but her parents knew that she was really married, and they were so heart-broken they never mentioned her name: They were Protestants and she had crossed the line and married a Catholic. But her mother often longed to see her.

When Darl prepared to leave home she told her youngest sister Annie the night before she left. She asked Annie to sleep in her room with her, claiming she was nervous.

When she came in for the evening, she found Annie already in bed and asleep: she awakened her and said, "Now Annie, I want you to take an oath on this Bible, not to tell what I'm going to tell you until tomorrow at dinner time when everyone is at the table."

"I promise"—said Annie.

"Annie," said Darl, "I am going away to marry Dare; I'm going to take the 5 o'clock train and Dare will meet me in Latrobe and we will be married in Pittsburgh. He has gotten a special dispensation from the priest Father Baldwin, and he went to Pittsburgh last night so as to draw some money from the bank and will come back as far as Latrobe to meet me."

Darl then turned to the packing of the suit cases, the next morning she crept out of the house and made her way to the station. She met no one on her way to the train, and as she had a mileage book she got on the train without being noticed by any one who knew her.

They were married and lived in Pittsburgh. Everything was lovely and life was one sweet dream. But one never-to-be-forgotten day

Royal lost his job and after many unsuccessful attempts succeeded in getting a position in Cleveland [where] they moved.

One day after eight months of a lonely time in Cleveland Darl wanted to move back to Pittsburgh. At first he refused: but when she pulled his head down and whispered a secret in his ear, he took her in his arms and kissed her, and said "anywhere my little 'Dream Face' where you will be happy."

Well, they moved back to Pittsburgh and Royal was happy in their expected happiness; but one day coming home unexpectedly he found his wife [unwell], with an illness that frightened him; she had always seemed well and healthy and you can judge his feelings when the [doctor] took him aside and whispered, epilepsy—brought on by excitement of some kind; he thought of his unborn babe and he was nearly crazy. After that spell Darl was never the same. Sometimes there were long intervals of happiness and Darl was her old self; then would come long dreary days of moroseness and sullenness, then everything went wrong and Darl [was] so dissatisfied, that Royal would think he would never be happy again. At last their baby was born. A bright healthy looking boy, and he thought their troubles were over.

But they had only commenced. Their baby was neglected and Darl would get the nurse to look after baby and house while she went to card parties, dances, afternoon teas or went autoing with some one of her numerous admirers.

Royal said to me one day, "Nurse I think there are moments in a man's life more bitter than the moments of death, more unendurable and more fatal." Such had come to Royal Dare, when he found his wife had betrayed his trust in her.

She had met her old lover Matt Walton, now Judge Walton, and he had become a frequent caller at their house in [Royal's] absence. [Royal] came home unexpectedly one day and found her in his arms, and said, "I lived a lifetime in a few moments, what they were, no words of mine can ever tell. I went up to her and touched her arm, she never moved and I turned to him, and I think for a few minutes I was mad, when I came to myself I was standing in the hall in my shirt sleeves and the betrayer of my home was lying on the pavement.

I shut the door and went back to my wife, the excitement had thrown her into another spell, I called the doctor and left the room, leaving her in his care. I shut myself up in my room and went through my agony alone. Three hours afterwards I returned to my wife's bedroom and found her still unconscious.

"I sat by her bedside until consciousness returned. I need not describe the scene that followed, suffice it to say three days afterwards I was alone, my wife had left me and took the baby with her."

Royal Dare never looked for his wife, as he judged — and rightly — that she was with Judge Walton.

His church recognized no divorce, and he wanted none, as he still loved his wife; so he kept his lonely home and went his lonely way, and at times longed for his wife and child back again.

One day she returned as unexpectedly as she had left, and said — without giving any explanation of her absence — I have returned home to stay, that and no more, and because of the love he could not kill, and that he still had for his child, he accepted her verdict; and as time passed, was again happy in his home life. He thought she had forgotten the past and he felt secure in her love for him at last.

But one long remembered evening he came home, and found her gone; not even a note to tell him where; he knew it was useless to hunt for her; but this time she had left behind the boy "Robert," still something he could shower his love on.

One week later, the news boys were crying the news on the street, "Strange Disappearance of Judge Walton of Somerville." No one connected his disappearance with that of any woman. Strange too, when they had been seen together so often; but so it was.

For months detectives scoured the country but they were not to be found, only Royal Dare or the Judge's bankers could have told the unhappy wife and children that their husband and father had deserted them even as he had been deserted.

Wife and children on one side, husband and child on the other, their only thoughts, loving ones, for those who had deserted them so basely.

When the Judge and Darl left they crossed the continent and plunged into all kinds of mad revelry. The woman held the man with a fine thread, and led him around as though he had no will; a whim, and nothing more. She took all and in return gave little, all forgotten or buried, only the present mattered.

One Christmas five years after the above happenings—Royal Dare received a telegram, and it contained only one line—"Come, your wife is dying."

Royal put his son in my care and went, only arriving in time to tell her, "he forgave her" and to close her eyes in death. He forgave, because he knew, she never knew, and never understood the gold she cast aside for the dross, or the lives she had wrecked in her search for pleasure.

Of Judge Walton "some of him lived, but most of him died, and when Royal Dare stood by his dead wife's side and looked at the wreck of the once brilliant man, who stood by his side, he thought his punishment was sufficient, I need add no more."

The judge took the first train back to Somerville which he reached three days later. The faithful wife greeted him without surprise, with love and joy filling her heart; where he had been she cared little, he was home again, and the years had marked him with scars that time might soften, but never could erase, they were seared too deep to erase; he had sown, he must reap.

Before he allowed her to say (this woman whom he should have loved and honored) "whether he could stay," he insisted—while she protested—in telling her of his life as he had lived it with Darl Dare.

He said "As you must remember the first time I was away from home, I was supposed to be away on court business; well the six months I was absent in Dixon, [Illinois], with Darl, who had her child with her. The child claimed too much of Darl's time and she left me one morning without a word of warning; three days later I received a letter saying, 'you have ceased to be amusing I have returned to Royal, and will not come back.' I was angry and I packed my grip and returned home.

"As you know, my work had accumulated rapidly, while I was away and I had to get down to work. I still thought I loved Darl and had determined now to pay her back, in her own coin. I thought I owed her double measure, because she played me false, once years ago, by eloping with Royal. My plan was to ruin Royal, and through him hurt her.

"I had to go to Pittsburgh and while there met her again one evening at the home of the judge I was stopping with or whose guest I was. She was an intimate friend of the judge's wife. Her old fascination over me was as strong as ever, and when I looked in her eyes, I forgot all else save the woman; time seemed to fly with her. When away from her I would form new resolutions, but they would all be forgotten when with her.

"Well when I left for home, we had made arrangements to leave everything and live only for each other. We went West and for a time everything was bright and beautiful. Darl had fairly done her best to keep me amused; then she commenced to tire of me, yet held me for her own pleasure and to satisfy every passing whim. Others fell under her spell and they were all served the same way, thrown aside when she tired of them.

"I have often prepared myself for flight, but her maid watched for her, and as I would think I'm free, she would appear before me, seemingly from nowhere, and laugh and taunt me, and when I would look at her my good resolutions all left me and when she said "come," I had not the will to do aught but what she said, and I would follow wherever she led. Once—in her absence—I started to telegraph you and as I finished writing it, she appeared, took it from me and tore it up. Did I stay at home often—No. We were constantly on the go; and were snubbed often by those whom she would have associated with, but nothing to her mattered, but fine clothes—wine—cards and self. When she became ill unto death she thought I was Royal, and died never knowing or understanding the harm she had done.

"I—poor fool have come to you a repentant broken man, whose oath for revenge fell back on his own head a thousand fold. See, Mary, I'm not even fit to touch the hem of your gown. Life holds nothing for me now but you and the children. When you have had time to consider, you may forgive and pity. I will go far away and live and try to help others to that which holds the better life.

"Tomorrow I will leave as I came and no scandal need be connected with you and the children, and when I return again, it will be only at your summons, and then not until I've earned your love and respect again and I will come—not a craven—but a MAN. I think I've been mad, but death has brought me to my senses, where I was blind now I see."

She put her hand on his bowed head, and said, "You have been cruel, cowardly and wicked, but you are kind now, and although you have made me suffer by your neglect, you did care for me once. We will go away together, and start life anew. I will forgive you fully and freely, if you will show to me that you can be a manly man—and will live to try to help others. God forgives the greatest of sins, and I can not sit in judgement on the father of my children."

Twenty years have passed and Royal Dare is happy once more, as this Christmas Day will bring him both great joy and love in plenty.

His son Robert brings to his home, this day of days, a wife and children. God has been good and he bows his head and thanks Him for the blessings bestowed upon him.

As I stand by Royal's chair, this joyous Christmas evening, his son takes his wife and children and points with pride to his mother's picture, and I hear Royal whisper, as he bows his head, "Thank God, he did not know and never will know THE WOMAN, who never could understand."

How I Won My Husband: A Christmas Story

∽

EVA S. PURDY

Eva S. Purdy

Eva S. Purdy, the daughter of John H. Murphy, a founder and the second editor of the *Baltimore Afro-American,* presents Christmas as a magical holiday, a time when all things are possible. Similar to Arline Weldon, the central character in "How I Won My Husband," Purdy was a middle-class African-American woman who enjoyed a life of privilege and who moved in what her contemporaries referred to as "the best of circles." This story reflects Purdy's perception of the lifestyle and issues that engaged some black middle-class women, as well as their struggle for recognition and independence within their families and communities.

Published by the *Baltimore Afro-American* in 1910, the plot for this story is set in a small mining town in the mountains of western Maryland at the beginning of the twentieth century. For Arline Weldon, Christmas is a very important time. It was the time when she met and married her husband, Clarence Pearson; it was the day her son was born; and it was the time she reunited with her family.

The story revolves around Arline, a teacher. Purdy uses Arline's character to express concern about both the devaluation of young women within the family and family expectations regarding young working women supporting the family. Arline, as did many young women of the time, feels that marriage will be an escape from the expectations and demands of her family. She decides that she will make her parents pay more attention and appreciate her more by getting married during the Christmas holidays. She is warned by Alice James, her good friend and fellow teacher, that marrying to escape family demands is not a good idea and that she might "marry in haste to repent at leisure."

Arline, however, does not give up easily and involves Alice in a deceptive plan to find a mate while visiting her married sister in New York City. Despite her well-earned reputation as a flirt, Arline manages to carry out her plan to attract and marry noted musician Clarence Pearson.

"How I Won My Husband" demonstrates the potential women have to control their lives. Purdy utilizes the character Arline to illustrate the power that women can have in structuring their lives. Arline refuses to be used by her parents as a means of family support and to wait for a man to find and marry her. She takes charge of her life and makes things happen.

How I Won My Husband: A Christmas Story

&

> "Love by no season bound is free!
> Not more the bird that sings,
> And soaring from its natal tree,
> With strong unfettered wings;
> Has liberty the world to roam.
> And make where'er he will a home!"

In a little town among the mountains of Western Maryland, two young women, who had been friends since childhood, taught school. The little mining town, like most others of its kind, nestled lazily in a valley surrounded by mountains.

The prettiest of the two women was standing thoughtfully by the window and though the sight outside was of magnificent beauty she saw it not. Snow covered mountains and trees, and everything, far as the eye could see, was one mass of ice and snow.

The moon was so bright and cold and cruel looking that Arline shivered. The wind that cried wildly down the streets and through the bright moonlight sky must have had some eerie force in it to make her start and shiver in spite of the blaze that sent such roseate flashes and shadows about the room. Certainly it was the awful suggestion of the wind, for there was nothing to shiver at in that comfortable little room, [with] Alice, her pretty little room-mate and friend.

Nothing stirred there save the flame and its shadows; there was no motion in the long folds of the curtains, no rustle in the leaves of the open book on Alice's lap. Now and then the fire snapped, the log sang, a bright coal dropped and dulled in the ashes, but that was all the life that seemed to be in the room.

At last Arline turned and looked at Alice who was dozing comfortably before the fire. Arline's gaze must have been very intent, because it made Alice restless, and looking up she caught her friend's intent look. She said: "Well Arline what's troubling you? You look uncanny enough to give a body the creeps; do sit down and don't stand there trying to look a body through and through like that," and the speaker, a pretty little brown eyed woman of two and twenty, looked really unhappy as she surveyed her friend who seemed from the pucker of her pretty mouth and the wrinkles in her forehead to be not over-pleased about something.

"Just read that postal card and you'll see what's the matter," and with a toss, she threw the card across to Alice.

Alice James read the card and then said: "Dear me, I don't see what's on this to worry one."

"You don't," snapped Arline. "Well I do. I've only read it once, and I know it by heart. Just listen and see if this isn't right."

" 'Dear Arline, have deferred my visit until later as Mary (that's my baby sister) has asked me to come up later, instead of the time I spoke of. I guess you are old enough to know what you want to do.

> Yours respectfully,
> WILFORD H. WELDON.' "

"Now would you take that to be from [my] father? No, I guess not; who would? Here I have been teaching for the past five years, and in all that time he has not deigned to pay me a visit. The only time he has been where I am is when business calls him; but then Mary is the youngest girl and of more account than I, though I can't see it.

"Jealous did you say? Well why shouldn't I be? I never hear from home only when money is needed or something wanted of me, and I remember the last time I was home for awhile, my mother told me distinctly if I could get anything to do, I had better do so, because there were so many children at home, she could not afford to keep me unless I paid board. Of course my money was pretty near all gone then, and that was as good as telling me I was not wanted.

"I sometime doubt if I belong to the Weldon family. I declare I feel positively devilish and I've made up my mind that I am going to do things, and I am going to make you all take notice. Now listen to me Alice James, school closes tomorrow for two weeks, the week to fix the furnace and Xmas week, and I am going to New York to visit my married sister, and I am going to get married, though I don't know to whom just yet, and —"

"But Arline you are such a flirt," interrupted Alice, "and how on earth you are going to manage to love a man and marry him in two weeks is more than I can understand. The very idea of a husband in two weeks, when you haven't met any one yet. You know the old saying: 'Marry in haste to repent at leisure.' You had better not try it."

"Don't prophesy any bad luck, Alice dear, because I am not going to fail. I want you to help me out."

"I — Oh indeed, Arline. I really can't do it."

"Oh yes you can my dear. You need not begin with your 'I can't,' because I generally manage to get my own way with other people, if I can't with home folks. That mother of mine hasn't written to me for a month, so I'll return the compliment and keep myself to myself."

"Arline, don't be so irreverent. You really should write to your mother. I can't think she means to slight you, and you know she has so much to do; please dear, don't talk so, you make me feel wretched."

"Really Alice, I can't imagine how you ever got courage to teach. Don't be so mealy mouthed. I told you before, I really feel up to doing something devilish, something to shock even your puritanical self, and I am going to have my way, so don't say any more about it, but sit still and listen.

"Now you are going with me; I've told my sister you are coming, so shut your little mouth."

"But Arline, my dear, I can't spare the money. I have so many Xmas gifts to give, and then again I have but one reception dress to my name."

"Alice James, you are the most provoking woman I know; money and dresses hasn't anything to do with this trip except to get your ticket. You know that everybody who knows Arline Weldon, calls her a heartless flirt. I am going to pick out a fellow when I get to New York, the one I am going to win, and I want to get some place near where he can hear me without my seeming to know he is near. I am going to have you with me, and I am going to say these words: 'It is no use Alice, I can't go home without Mr. — — — knowing I love him. What will I do? Everybody says I am such a heartless flirt that I know he has heard it ere this; but I am really in earnest. I love him with all my heart and soul. I love him so dearly that if I had to die, when I got to heaven, I would worry them with my ceaseless cries and the questions I would ask about him, that they would find him and bring him to me.' If he really cares for me at all, at that point he will appear, and you must disappear and leave us together. In plain words I am going to propose, but as it is not leap year, I can't do so openly."

"But Arline I'll be sure to forget and laugh, it all sounds so superbly ridiculous."

"Alice James I solemnly swear if you do such a thing I'll never speak to you again."

Friday night following this conversation between Arline and Alice, found them both in the city of New York.

"Alice," exclaimed Arline, "this is Friday isn't it?"

"Yes dear, why?"

"Because this is the night of Mrs. Lea's reception, and I hear that Clarence Pearson, the great violinist, has returned from a tour through Europe, and is expected to be there. I am going to wear pure white tonight, and not a jewel of any kind, my favorite you know, and if I don't capture the prize tonight you need never claim Arline Weldon as your dearest friend again." And with a gay laugh Arline danced out of the room.

The ball and reception was the swellest function of the season, and Arline was the belle of the evening; in that gay throng, she was the gayest of the gay; beautiful, brilliant and witty, she captured all hearts; but she was not satisfied. The expected guest had not yet arrived, but at last he came. Arline saw him as he entered and greeted his hostess, and as she passed Alice she whispered hurriedly: "Alice, Oh Alice, the lion of the day is here."

It did not take Clarence long to discover Arline. He heard her talked of on every hand, and though no matter how much any one praised her they always ended with the words: "But such a heartless flirt." Nevertheless he was attracted to her, and at last asked a friend to introduce [her].

"Hard hit, old fellow?" asked Carl Bradley. "It's no use, she'll only send you to the right about as she has dozens of others."

"Never mind," said Clarence, "I'll risk it."

"Miss Weldon," said Carl Bradley, "my friend desires to meet you." And as he presented Clarence, Arline extended her hand with usual frankness, and showed that she was genuinely pleased to meet him.

As Clarence acknowledged the introduction, he looked at her sweet face and thought her one of the most beautiful women he had ever met, and he vowed to himself, then and there, that he would win her for his own if he could.

Her white dress, though plain and unadorned, only served to heighten the exquisite purity of her complexion. Her eyes were like black diamonds. She was a rarely beautiful woman, with hair like spun gold and eyes as black as sloes with a complexion that rivaled a peach. As to her manners they were perfect; she was frank, unaffected and with all perfectly refined, a woman to love and be loved.

As Alice and Arline were bidding their hostess good evening, Clarence stood waiting to accompany them to their carriage, as he bade them good night he managed to whisper quickly to Arline.

"May I call tomorrow afternoon, if you will be at home."

She answered: "Yes, between three and four. Good night." With a nod and a slight pressure of her hand, he closed the door and was soon lost in the darkness of the night.

The days following were the happiest Arline and Clarence had ever known. He was her shadow. He managed to find out where she was going and would always be there also. People shook their heads and smiled, but all exclaimed: "Only another flirtation, what a pity."

"Alice," said Arline about a week afterwards, "you know we must leave here for the mountains the last of the week. Clarence calls this afternoon, and I've been wondering how to carry my plans out. Sister will be out visiting, and as Lizzie is to keep house, I will inform her I am going across the street to see Myra Lovell, and if any one calls to come after us. Of course I am not going out of the house; but when Lizzie goes across the street for us, we'll both be in the room adjoining the parlor, and not supposed to know he has been admitted to the house. Please don't forget the part you are to play, and I assure you unless I am much deceived you will be bridesmaid for your harum-scarum old friend [before] two more days roll over your head."

When Clarence Pearson called, he was wondering to himself if she loved him or could love him, and if he could trust her. He loved her dearly, but she was termed such a heartless flirt that he was half afraid to ask her, yet he could not bring himself to believe she was heartless; a flirt she might be, but not heartless.

As the door bell rang the girls slipped into the sitting room and commenced to talk, and when Lizzie after inviting Clarence into the parlor, and telling him she would go for the ladies—they were only across the street—left the house, Clarence heard voices quite distinctly.

He started to cough to let them know of his presence when he heard his name spoken by Arline and her declaration of love for himself.

After Arline had finished, Alice said: "Mr. Pearson does not love you, and if he did he could not marry you before Friday. Today is Tuesday and you'll have to return home with out your Prince Charming."

"No she won't either," and at that both girls jumped to their feet, and Arline blushing prettily exclaimed:

"Oh Mr. Pearson, what must you think of us? We did not know any one was in the house."

Taking her in his arms and kissing her he told her he thought she was the sweetest and best little woman in the whole wide world, and if she would consent, they would go quietly over in Jersey City Wednesday morning and be married.

In the meantime Alice had gone to her room, and was wondering if Arline was really in love with Clarence and if she intended to marry him. She was not left long in doubt. About one-half hour afterwards Arline came into the room and told her she was expected to go with them in the morning as she was to be married and she must not tell a living soul.

When the marriage was read in Saturday's *Afro-American Ledger* it created a perfect sensation, and congratulations poured in on the young couple.

At first Mr. and Mrs. Weldon refused to own their daughter. But the young couple were too much infatuated with each other to care about what any one thought. They took a trip West and spent six weeks among friends and then returned to Baltimore, Arline's home, and settled down quietly in the dearest little home imaginable. A happier couple it would be hard to find.

Mrs. Pearson never tires of telling how she won her husband. She is perfectly happy in her husband's and young son's love, and every Christmas she has three things to be happy for, Clarence, Jr., who was born on Christmas day, and the reconciliation with her parents, which took place the same day she gave them a little grandson, and the last but not least the love and husband she first met on a merry Christmas night.

Papa's postal card is their dearest treasure. It is framed and hangs on the wall as a valuable treasure; because if it had not been for the card she would not thought of playing such a trick. It caused her to win the very best of husbands.

Arline says "as Clarence laughs as heartily as I over the trick, I am not ashamed to tell any one how I won my husband."

It Came to Pass:
A Christmas Story

❧

BRUCE L. REYNOLDS

Bruce L. Reynolds

"It Came to Pass," published in December 1939 in the *Chicago Defender*, is a traditional Christmas story that reinforces the power of religious faith, a cornerstone in African-American history and culture. In the words of the Apostle Paul, "Faith is the substance of things hoped for, the evidence of things not seen." It is a belief that God's power is infinite. In this story, Edward and Ella, an elderly couple beset by poverty, lacking food, and unable to obtain decent medical care, are uplifted by their deep love for one another and their abiding faith in God.

The story opens on Christmas Eve in a large northern city, whose public spaces reflect the beauty and opulence of Christmas frequently seen in the business sections of large urban centers. Reynolds juxtaposes the luxury reflected in the private and public celebratory displays of Christmas with the abject poverty and suffering of people like Edward and Ella. He demonstrates that there are two worlds—one the highly visible world of privilege and one the obscure world of despair and suffering.

Although no biographical data on Bruce Reynolds accompanied the publication of this story, he is clearly a product of the Harlem Renaissance period and, like many African-Americans, seems to have been deeply religious. By December 1939, a time when Europe was beset by war and America was in the grips of the Depression, it appeared that many people had forgotten God. Reynolds reminds the reader that God is real, and that he answers prayers.

Edward and Ella represent the deep and transcending faith of African-Americans, who historically survived the terrors of the Middle Passage, the horrors of slavery, the unremitting struggle to survive poverty, lynching, and mental and physical abuse, and who fervently believed that God would also see them through the Depression. During a time of great poverty and despair, Reynolds reinforced the message of faith and hope in God.

It Came to Pass: A Christmas Story

୭ର

It was Christmas Eve. The city was covered with a fresh blanket of crunchy, white snow, and more was falling. Christmas wreaths hung in windows and on doors. Passersby could glimpse many a brightly-lighted and tinseled tree. In the public park was a Christmas tree that dwarfed the humans who clustered around its base, singing carols. In the metropolitan section, a skyscraper office building had formed a striking cross with lighted windows. The clamor of church bells mingled with the stately, beautiful melody of "Silent Night, Holy Night," as played on a giant carillon in a nearby university. Hearts, unfeeling throughout a rather hectic year, were bursting with good will and good cheer and gratitude.

But it was another story in two bare, chilly basement rooms. In one of the rooms and ill [in] a bed, lay an old lady. Her suffering had pulled in her cheeks, and her eyes were like burning coals deep in two dark wells. At her bedside sat an elderly man in tattered clothes. He squinted through oval shaped glasses at an open Bible on his knees.

And now he turned his eyes to the still face of his wife of nearly forty-two years.

"I can't read any more, Ella," he told her wearily. He closed the Bible disconsolately. "With so much going on in the world—war and the like—seems like we've slipped God's mind. I'm not blaming anybody or anything, Ella. But when I think of all the money spent for tomorrow, I get a little shaky knowing we have about a dollar. Of course, we'll get our basket tomorrow. Goodness knows I'm grateful for kind hearted folks. But you won't be able to eat anything, Ella. It'll be the first time we have not eaten together on Christmas."

Ella turned her head slowly to face him. "I'm sorry to spoil things, Edward." Her voice was just a whisper. "But I can't seem to hold a thing on my stomach."

"If you only had decent medical treatment," old Edward muttered. "The city doctor is all right. But he admits there isn't much he can do. Besides, he has so many calls to make, he can't take up much time with any one patient. Oh, Ella, if we could only get that specialist, Dr. Wayne, to come out. I know he could do something. The city doctor said he could. He's the best in the city."

Ella closed her eyes. "But he's a rich doctor. They say he charges five dollars a visit. He has no time for poverty stricken old folks like us. You called him twice. Each time he flatly refused to see me."

"Yes. He told us to see the city doctor."

There was a knock on the door. Edward looked quizzically at his wife.

"Wonder who that is?"

"Maybe it's that nice couple down the street, Edward."

He went to the door and opened it. A man stood smiling. He carried a small bag in one hand.

"You've been trying to contact Dr. Wayne," the man said, coming in. He opened his coat to shake off the snow. "I have come. Where is the patient?"

Old Edward fell upon his knees at the man's feet. "Thank God you've come, Dr. Wayne. Everybody seems to think you can do what others can't." He rose. "Let me help you out of your coat." He touched the doctor's arm.

Dr. Wayne shook his head. "That won't be necessary."

Old Edward jerked his hand back as though he had touched a live wire. For a moment he stared incredulously into the doctor's eyes. The uncertain light from a lamp fell across the doctor's face, revealing that his eyes were his most singular feature. They baffled description. They were not like eyes, it seemed. Rather, more like windows, across which a veil had been drawn.

"You wait here," Dr. Wayne told the old man. He went into Ella's room and closed the door.

Edward sat down and waited. That look of incredulity was still on his face. What manner of man was this Dr. Wayne? He had no sense of time. But he got to his feet when the doctor came out of Ella's room.

"Your wife wants to see you," he said. "Don't worry about tomorrow. She will be able to eat with you."

"How did you know—"

"Just keep faith in your heart. Nourish it, cherish it until it reflects in your thinking and dreaming and doing."

"What a strange thing for a doctor to say," Edward murmured.

"But not strange for me," the doctor said. "And now I must be going. Merry Christmas to you."

With that, he opened the door and was gone. Edward looked down at the steps leading out of his basement rooms. He blinked his eyes hard. Grass seemed to be growing out of the doctor's footsteps in the snow! Edward closed the door and hurried to his wife's side. He found her sitting up in bed, reading the Bible. She had not been able to sit up in bed for three months! He fell upon his knees by the bed.

"Ella—Ella, who was that?"

She smiled at him. "What does your heart tell you? You saw his eyes, Edward. You see me now."

"I touched his arm, Ella," he remembered. "I saw grass growing in the snow where he walked. Ella—"

Some carolers were singing outside. It was "Joy To The World." Understanding dawned upon Edward. His eyes filled as he found

Ella's hand. Their faces were radiant. Their eyes met in mutual and glorious acknowledgment.

"He came to our bare rooms to give us the greatest Christmas gift of all."

"Yes, Edward. But remember, he was born in a manger."

A Christmas Journey

LOUIS LORENZO REDDING

Louis Lorenzo Redding

Louis Lorenzo Redding was born in Alexandria, Virginia, in 1901, and grew up in Wilmington, Delaware. In 1923 he received an undergraduate degree from Brown University and subsequently taught English at Morehouse College in Atlanta. At the time he wrote "A Christmas Journey," he was a graduate student at Harvard University Law School. Among the first of his race to graduate from the law school, in 1929 Redding became the first African-American admitted to the bar in Delaware. Beginning as an attorney in private practice, Redding later worked with the NAACP Legal Defense and Educational Fund and as a public defender in Wilmington.

A pioneer in the fight for the desegregation of schools and housing, in 1950 Redding represented nine African-American students at Delaware State College who wanted to attend the all-white University of Delaware. Pursuing this case, he won two landmark decisions, *Parker* v. *the University of Delaware* and

Bulah/Belton v. *Bebhart*, which provided the legal basis for deseg-regation in Delaware. These decisions were forerunners of the famous *Brown* v. *Board of Education of Topeka, Kansas* case that led to the desegregation of the nation's public schools, and they also served as catalysts for legislation ending segregation and dis-crimination in housing, voting, public transportation, and public facilities.

Redding, whose life and work were motivated by the belief that the best way to achieve racial equality was through the pas-sage of laws, used social realism to explore the meaning of Christmas for the dispossessed. "A Christmas Journey," pub-lished in *Opportunity* in December 1925, reflects the pessimism and chaos that was so evident in the period following World War I. Redding employs the Christmas theme to bring attention to societal ills that he felt needed to be addressed.

Set in Boston, "A Christmas Journey" is the story of Jim and Elsie, two individuals whose lives have been led in the margins of mainstream society. Jim, a white man, is described as an incur-able consumptive who knows that death is near. Elsie is a very light complexioned African-American woman who is passing for white. These two characters are bonded by their love in a common-law marriage. Through their lives and their reflections on life, Redding explores social issues such as interracial marriage, the social impact of tuberculosis, and society's indifference to human suffering.

Redding forces the reader to reflect upon the real meaning of Christmas: loving, sharing, and caring for others. He suggests that for many people Christmas has become just another holiday to engage in consumerism. As Jim observes the hustle and bustle of Christmas Eve shoppers, he describes them as "Fools . . . poor, ignorant fools, to whom life is a dollar, a loaf of hard bread, an imitation diamond, a suit of shoddy, woolen underwear! Preparing to celebrate Christmas! Bah! What do they know about Christmas—or what do they care? It's just another holiday to them!"

Although Redding demonstrates the callousness and lack of concern that permeates the Christmas celebration in a large urban center, he overlooks several central themes that have fueled mankind's existence for centuries, and which force us to reflect on the meaning of Christmas and life. Christmas in the best of traditions represents a rebirth of life. It holds out the possibility for change. It stresses faith, hope, and love. Jim and Elsie, feeling disconnected from society, embrace the cynicism of the time and abandon their faith and hope. In the end they are left with only their love for one another.

A Christmas Journey

∾

For Love the master symphonist
Ignoring [vanity], creed and hue,
Mocks dicta that stifle and twist
To give consonant souls their due.

The raw sting of the cold, night air struck the consumptive's [shrunken] chest. He gasped, coughed, gasped again, and with a slender hand, quivering from the exertion of his coughing, drew up the collar of his overcoat.

"This thing's got me all right! That fool of an army doctor! A lot he knew about gas! And he told me that I'd wear it off in a few months! Wear it off! Well, it'll soon be off now — but not in the way he said."

Abstractedly he had taken his habitual route homeward. It led through the street market, which was thronged with Christmas-eve buyers, stocking up for the season that the morrow would usher in.

The air was full of shrill babel and of the fresh smell of raw foodstuffs; the street was a jumble of motley wares. Nowhere else in great Boston could be found more eloquent proof of the cosmopolitanism of the city. Improvised signs in Yiddish, Italian, and Spanish, as well as in English, leered at the purchasers from all angles. Creeping, pipe-puffing Chinese with American overcoats over their loose native jackets bought greens from Italian merchants. Buxom Irish housewives bought red meat from German butchers. Greeks, Negroes, Poles— everybody, bought a great variety of things from that ubiquitous merchant, the Jew. Peanuts and cabbages, carrots and shoestrings, turkeys and bandannas, trousers and cheap jewelry, silk stockings and codfish—all were bargained for with equal gusto. Here, verily, was a paradise for the poor; but despite the low prices, no sale was complete without haggling.

The consumptive, as he weakly jostled his way through the alien melange, saw nothing that interested him. He was more than sated with the world. He loathed everything, even the scrawny, yellow fowl that a red-bearded Jew was swinging in the air and offering for sale in a rasping falsetto. Nor did he mask his contemptuous feelings under a hypocritical look of complacency; his wan countenance was frankly sardonic.

"Fools," he muttered between coughs, "poor, ignorant fools, to whom life is a dollar, a loaf of hard bread, an imitation diamond, a suit of shoddy, woolen underwear! Preparing to celebrate Christmas! Bah! What do they know about Christmas—or what do they care? It's just another holiday for them!"

A heavy foreign sounding voice sang out:

"Dancin' monkeys here, only a quarter. Git a dancin' monkey."

The words shattered the cynical musings of the consumptive and sent a train of incoherent and confused images swirling through his brain.

"Dancin' monkeys—"

The sound came with haunting urgency and the man moved toward the spot from which it seemed to come. He beheld a short, unkempt, alien seeming peddler standing at the edge of the curb. On the ground beside him was a huge basket filled with bits of painted metal. In one hand the peddler held a string from the end of which dangled a monkey, crudely fashioned in tin, with a red coat and black trousers painted on his body in burlesque of the apparel of man. While the peddler lustily proclaimed his toy, he pulled the string and the monkey hopped and jumped, spun and danced. Occasionally a passer-by ventured from the main current of the crowd to look and pass on, but rarely to buy. There was no fascination for the consumptive in the terpsichorean efforts of the monkey, but he did find himself interested in the degree of imbecility that could cause anyone to invest money in such a glittering, senseless bauble. He looked at the bawling vendor with a feeling of contempt not unmixed with pity. "Why doesn't he get a real job? Anything would be more profitable than this."

But there was no answer in the loud cry of the peddler. . . . Again the emaciated man looked at the dangling monkey. He noted its gaudy, man-like costume; he watched its poor pantomime of human dancing; and he looked again at the man who held the string. The latter's eyes were bright with a far-seeing lustre.

"Ah!" thought the consumptive. "This peddler is a dreamer and a cynic. Perhaps he finds a peculiar significance in this profitless business of selling monkeys. He sees in his painted monkey the likeness of its higher analogue, man. To the peddler, perhaps, the monkey daubed with its thin coating of paint is man, smeared with the thin veneer of civilization. This mettlesome hopping and jumping, spinning and dancing of the monkey represents man, the puppet, fuming turbulently under the strings held by king and war-lord, exploiter and slave-driver. Just as here and there on the monkey a gleam of brightness reveals the metal, untouched by the paint; so too with man, whose soul-devouring passions and prejudices, whose avarice and blood-thirst reveal his baser self, untouched by the dissembling veneer of civilization."

Suddenly the string snapped. The crazy gewgaw tottered defiantly a second, and then fell ungracefully to the snow-covered pavement.

"Aha! Aha! The monkey won't dance! He's broken his string!

That's what we've done—Elsie and I. We've broken the fettering strings of society and are resolved to dance no longer!"

The consumptive moved on. He had promised Elsie that he would return to her early. Near the end of the market block there were booths where cedar trees and holly were sold. The wholesome Christmas aroma came to him, and he stopped, searched through several pockets, and having collected all of his change, bought the largest holly wreath he saw. The purchase of the wreath was an unreasoned action; it simply completed a reflex caused by the stimulation of the man's olfactory nerve centers by the cedars and holly.

Where the market ended, the street was narrow and dim-lit. Ugly, old brick houses, the cellars of which quartered a heterogeneous array of tradesmen's mean shops, lined the street. In many of the windows above the shops were lighted candles. Some windows, uncurtained, revealed women and children decking Christmas trees. After a time the man with the wreath turned into a street yet darker and meaner and flanked with tall houses which made it seem more narrow than it was. Here there were no shops, nor were there windows from which candles shone. The consumptive crept over the crisp snow, and then he entered a house, passed through the black hallway, and groped his way up a flight of resounding, bare stairs. He paused at the first landing to recover his panting breath. He listened to his labored breathing as it rattled ominously in the frosty air; and there in the darkness, he smiled. Then, after climbing wearily the remaining three flights, he opened a door and entered a long room, which offered a sudden antithesis to anything the dismal appearance of the street would have presaged.

The room was well carpeted and was warmed by an open hearth. A reading lamp on a sturdy oaken table cast its glow over books and magazines lying there. In one corner, where the light but faintly reached, the blackness of a low piano blended with the shadows. The farther end of the room was screened off. The consumptive went behind the screens. There in an ancient, wooden bed beneath snowy covers a woman was sleeping lightly. The brilliancy of her abundant, black hair enhanced the white purity of its background. Her face, half-clouded by a capricious shadow, was composed and untroubled. Suddenly, as if informed by some strange telepathy of the watcher beside her bed, she awoke and gazed up into his haggard face.

"Jim," she said, "did the druggist let you have it?"

"Yes, Elsie. It was easy. How do you feel?"

"Rested now, Jim. What's that? Oh, holly! It's only a few hours before Christmas, isn't it? Do you know, Jim, that I was born just thirty years ago tomorrow, on Christmas Day?"

"No, I didn't know it, dear. We've never talked birthdays, but I could have guessed that you were born on Christmas or Easter or on some Holy Day."

"Holy Day, Jim? No, Jim. There are no days holy in themselves; they're all alike unless people hallow them in their hearts and consciences. But most people don't hallow them inwardly. They use meaningless symbols like that holly wreath."

He hung the wreath on a post at the foot of the bed, and then took from his pocket two packages and placed them on a small table beside the bed. The woman saw the packages and her somber eyes sparkled.

"What's the larger package, Jim?"

"The bottle? Oh, that's champagne from Champagne, or as we had to call it when on furloughs from Hell, 'Du vin blanc.' " And he smiled weakly, and began feverishly to unbutton his overcoat.

But the eyes of woman are all-seeing; moreover, her intuition is mercurial and unerring.

"What's the trouble, Jim?"

"Nothing, dear. What makes you ask?"

"You're not as confident as when you went out. You seem excited."

"It's nothing. But, Elsie, I've been thinking about things, and about you. I've been wondering whether you have ever really cared that we weren't legally married."

"Oh, Jim! Why do you ask me that? No, I've never cared. I've never really thought about marriage. There were too many difficulties. Even if you had been well, our life would have been chiefly with ourselves. Marriage, too, would have been too sensational. The officials would have detected that I'm not white, and if they hadn't I couldn't lie about it. I would have told. And then, Jim, just imagine the newspaper stories and the editorials ranting of intermarriage and—"

"Don't, Elsie, don't! The fools who write newspapers don't know that in reality any marriage is an intermarriage. There must be some interchange, some blending, whether it be of dissimilar blood or of other qualities. I love you because you have every spiritual quality that I don't have, and because you are beautiful, because you are loyal, because your voice is gentle and soft, because your music charms me. You've been what any real mate is—a complement. As for the newspapers, had I been a well man, and had you wanted marriage, that would have come first, despite newspapers or anything else. As it was, I had no right to ask you to tie yourself to a weak and gloomy skeleton."

He stopped. Elsie was gazing steadfastly at him, and he continued:

"But this illness has changed my ideas; indeed—who knows—it may have clarified them, for now I hate the world that would deny me honest happiness after making me a weakling. God! How I detest men's pharisaic exactions and their smug conceits! I don't see how I could bring myself now to stoop to even one of their conventions.

"And, Elsie, you've been my comforter. You've listened to my ravings and quieted them. You've saved me from genuine misery and folly. And all this you've done for a wreck—a mere broken clod."

"Don't brood, Jim. You must not."

"I don't mean to, Elsie; but I've been thinking that it isn't fair to persuade you to do this—to go with me if you're not altogether willing."

"It's all settled now, Jim. I've been thinking too while you were away, and I now know that I don't want to do anything else—and I won't do anything else."

Reverently, Jim bent down and kissed her smooth forehead. Then, as if not completely assured, he said:

"If you're not sure, Elsie, I can go alone."

"Never mind, Jim: we're going together. I won't be separated from you. It's not your fault things haven't gone well. It's just been Fate."

Then, as if motivated by some slow passion welling up from the depths of his spirit, Jim again bent over the bed and kissed the woman, not quickly, or impulsively, but deliberately, first her forehead, then her cheeks and her lips.

He turned away and with head bowed walked beyond the screens. . . .

When he returned, he sat on the edge of the bed. The woman drew close and he enclosed her in his arm.

"Do you know, Jim, this has been a glorious experience—just two of us, living one for the other with nothing else to live for? I sometimes think that neither of us would have been happy if Fate had kept us apart. The sanction of the world for us, and for all like us, is only fair, but I doubt, Jim, if sanction could have made us any happier. . . . I wonder if the newspapers will get our story? Yes, I can see it now, headlines and all!"

"I don't mind that, Elsie. The thing that I don't like is that I don't know what will be done with us, going in this way."

"What's found won't be us, Jim, dear. But let's not worry these few minutes. Let's not even talk. Let's just think and be happy."

She nestled closer as if she thought that physical touch would foster that spiritual communion that she desired.

He was content. Whatever doubt he had as to the fairness of taking her with him was overcome by her earnest and tender devotion. She would have it no other way. She was his now and eternally. . . .

An hour passed, and bells, not sweet-toned from some rich temple, but harsh and mechanical began tolling the Christmas tide in.

"Are you ready, Jim?" she whispered.

"Yes, dear. Are you?"

"Yes," she murmured.

He reached to the table beside the bed for the smaller package. As he shook its contents into a glass, he smiled at the grinning death's-head the red label blazoned. There was a delightful tinkling sound as the champagne bottle in his weak and shaking hand kissed the rim of the glass into which the liquid gurgled.

He handed her the glass, and with his free arm drew her close to him.

She drank.

He took the glass, drank, and dropped it.

The bells rang on. . . .

They were drowsy now, but still conscious. Their embrace tightened.

The bells ceased.

One Christmas Eve

❧

LANGSTON HUGHES

Langston Hughes

Langston Hughes was born in Joplin, Missouri, in 1902. His grandfather had been a radical abolitionist, his mother had a predilection for acting and writing poetry, and his father studied law. Gaining recognition in 1921 for writing "The Negro Speaks of Rivers," his most celebrated poem, he became one of the most acclaimed of the poets, novelists, and dramatists of the twentieth century. Hughes published at least nine volumes of poetry, including *The Weary Blues* (1926), *Fine Clothes to the Jew* (1927), *The Dream Keeper and Other Poems* (1932), *Shakespeare in Harlem* (1942), *Fields of Wonder* (1947), *One Way Ticket* (1949), *Montage of a Dream Deferred* (1951), *Ask Your Mama: 12 Moods for Jazz* (1961), and *The Panther and the Lash* (1967). His fiction was published in six novels —*Not Without Laughter* (1930), *Simple Speaks His Mind* (1950), *Simple Takes a Wife* (1953), *Simple Stakes a Claim* (1957), *Tambourines to Glory* (1958), and *Simple's Uncle Sam* (1965) —and three volumes of short stories —*The Ways of White Folks* (1934),

Laughing to Keep from Crying (1952), and *Something in Common and Other Stories* (1963).

"One Christmas Eve" was published in *Opportunity* in December 1933. The editor noted that "Langston Hughes, just returned from a lengthy stay in Russia, turns his hand to the short story and shows a growing mastery of that medium." Prior to going to the Soviet Union in 1932, at the insistence of noted educator Mary McLeod Bethune, Hughes traveled throughout the South reading to mainly black audiences. Listening to the stories of black southerners and experiencing segregation and discrimination at every hand inspired Hughes to write "One Christmas Eve."

In 1930 the majority of African-American women workers were employed as domestics. In many small Southern towns, such as the one described by Hughes, educated and uneducated African-American women and men had few economic opportunities. The majority, many without formal education, worked as servants and in agriculture. Teaching and preaching were the primary professional employments open to educated blacks. Arcie, the central character of this story, personifies the plight of some black servants, and of many African-American women who worked to support their families. Arcie, a single woman with a young child, works long hours for meager wages, which barely support her basic needs. Yet, with all of her problems, she struggles to provide her child with a "normal" Christmas.

Hughes demonstrates Arcie's efforts to make Christmas a happy occasion for Joe, her five-year-old son, and employs the Christmas theme to illustrate the vast economic gap between whites and blacks, and the lack of concern evidenced by some whites about the lives of their servants. Like John Henrik Clarke in "Santa Claus Is a White Man," Hughes examines the meaning of Santa Claus for black children, especially boys.

Hughes's Santa Claus, like Clarke's, does not see Joe simply as a child, who like all children, idolizes Santa and believes in his goodness. For Santa Claus, Joe is just a Negro—a reviled figure to be made fun of, an animal without humanity, and a beast of burden to be used. Like all children who gravitate toward Santa Claus, Joe sees no reason why he should not enter the lobby of a segregated movie theater where Santa is dispensing gifts and good cheer.

Because of the particular vulnerability of black males to lynching and other racial attacks, Hughes and Clarke used black boys to demonstrate the problem black parents faced in trying to provide a "normal" childhood for their children while at the same time educating them about what it meant to be black in America. The dilemma African-American parents, particularly Southern blacks, confronted each December was how to celebrate and embrace the traditional definition of Christmas and Santa Claus and at the same time protect their children from the dangers posed by racism, inherent in every aspect of United States culture—even Christmas.

One Christmas Eve

∾

Standing over the hot stove cooking supper, the colored maid, Arcie, was very tired. Between meals today, she had cleaned the whole house for the white family she worked for, getting ready for Christmas tomorrow. Now her back ached and her head felt faint from sheer fatigue. Well, she would be off in a little while, if only the Missus and her children would come on home to dinner. They were out shopping for more things for the tree which stood all ready, tinsel-hung and lovely in the living room, waiting for its candles to be lighted.

Arcie wished she could afford a tree for Joe. He'd never had one yet, and it's nice to have such things when you're little. Joe was five, going on six. Arcie, looking at the roast in the white folks' oven, wondered how much she could afford to spend tonight on toys for Joe. She only got seven dollars a week, and four of that went for her room and the landlady's daily looking after Joe while Arcie was at work.

"Lord, it's more'n a notion raisin' a child," she thought.

She looked at the clock on the kitchen table. After seven. What made white folks so inconsiderate, she wondered. Why didn't they come on home here to supper? They knew she wanted to get off before all the stores closed. She wouldn't have time to buy Joe nothin' if they didn't hurry. And her landlady probably wanting to go out and shop, too, and not be bothered with little Joe.

"Doggone it!" Arcie said to herself. "If I just had my money, I might leave the supper on the stove for 'em. I just got to get to the stores fo' they close." But she hadn't been paid for the week yet. The Missus had promised to pay her Christmas Eve, a day or so ahead of time.

Arcie heard a door slam and talking and laughter in the front of the house. She went in and saw the Missus and her kids shaking snow off their coats.

"Umm-m! It's swell for Christmas Eve," one of the kids said to Arcie. "It's snowin' like the deuce, and mother came near driving through a stop light. Can't hardly see for the snow. It's swell!"

"Supper's ready," Arcie said. She was thinking how her shoes weren't very good for walking in snow.

It seemed like the white folks took as long as they could to eat that evening. While Arcie was washing dishes, the Missus came out with her money.

"Arcie," the Missus said, "I'm so sorry, but would you mind if I just gave you five dollars tonight? The children have made me run short of change, buying presents and all."

"I'd like to have seven," Arcie said. "I needs it."

"Well, I just haven't got seven," the Missus said. "I didn't know you'd want all your money before the end of the week, anyhow. I just haven't got it to spare."

Arcie took five. Coming out of the hot kitchen, she wrapped up as well as she could and hurried by the house where she roomed to get little Joe. At least he could look at the Christmas trees in the windows downtown.

The landlady, a big light yellow woman, was in a bad humor. She said to Arcie, "I thought you was comin' home early and get this child. I guess you know I want to go out, too, once in a while."

Arcie didn't say anything, for if she had, she knew the landlady would probably throw it up to her that she wasn't getting paid to look after a child both night and day.

"Come on, Joe," Arcie said to her son, "Let's us go in the street."

"I hears they got a Santa Claus downtown," Joe said, wriggling into his worn little coat. "I want to see him."

"Don't know 'bout that," his mother said, "But hurry up and get your rubbers on. Stores'll be closed directly."

It was six or eight blocks downtown. They trudged along through the falling snow, both of them a little cold. But the snow was pretty!

The main street was hung with bright red and blue lights. In front of the City Hall there was a Christmas tree — but it didn't have no presents on it, only lights. In the store windows there were lots of toys—for sale.

Joe kept on saying, "Mama, I want. . . ."

But mama kept walking ahead. It was nearly ten, when the stores were due to close, and Arcie wanted to get Joe some cheap gloves and something to keep him warm, as well as a toy or two. She thought she might come across a rummage sale where they had children's clothes. And in the ten-cent store, she could get some toys.

"O-oo! Lookee . . . ," little Joe kept saying, and pointing at things in the windows. How warm and pretty the lights were, and the shops, and the electric signs through the snow.

It took Arcie more than a dollar to get Joe's mittens and things he needed. In the A & P Arcie bought a big box of hard candies for 49 cents. And then she guided Joe through the crowd on the street until they came to the dime store. Near the ten-cent store they passed a moving picture theatre. Joe said he wanted to go in and see the movies.

Arcie said, "Ump-un! No, child. This ain't Baltimore where they have shows for colored, too. In these here small towns, they don't let colored folks in. We can't go in there."

"Oh," said little Joe.

In the ten-cent store, there was an awful crowd. Arcie told Joe to stand outside and wait for her. Keeping hold of him in the crowded store would be a job. Besides she didn't want him to see what toys she was buying. They were to be a surprise from Santa Claus tomorrow.

Little Joe stood outside the ten-cent store in the light, and the snow, and people passing. Gee, Christmas was pretty. All tinsel and stars and cotton. And Santa Claus a-coming from somewhere, dropping things in stockings. And all the people in the streets were carrying things, and the kids looked happy.

But Joe soon got tired of just standing and thinking and waiting in front of the ten-cent store. There were so many things to look at in the other windows. He moved along up the block a little, and then a little more, walking and looking. In fact, he moved until he came to the picture show.

In the lobby of the moving picture show, behind the plate glass doors, it was all warm and glowing and awful pretty. Joe stood looking in, and as he looked his eyes began to make out, in there blazing beneath holly and colored streamers and the electric stars of the lobby, a marvelous Christmas tree. A group of children and grown-ups, white, of course, were standing around a big man in red beside the tree. Or was it a man? Little Joe's eyes opened wide. No, it was not a man at all. It was Santa Claus!

Little Joe pushed open one of the glass doors and ran into the lobby of the white moving picture show. Little Joe went right through the crowd and up to where he could get a good look at Santa Claus. And

Santa Claus was giving away gifts, little presents for children, little boxes of animal crackers and stick-candy canes. And behind him on the tree was a big sign, (which little Joe didn't know how to read). It said, to those who understood, *Merry Christmas from Santa Claus to our young patrons.* Around the lobby, other signs said, *When you come out of the show stop with your children and see our Santa Claus.* And another announced, *Gem Theatre makes its customers happy—see our Santa.*

And there was Santa Claus in a red suit and a white beard all sprinkled with tinsel snow. Around him were rattles and drums and rocking horses which he was not giving away. But the signs on them said (could little Joe have read) that they would be presented from the stage on Christmas Day to the holders of lucky numbers. Tonight, Santa Claus was only giving away candy, and stick-candy canes, and animal crackers to the kids.

Joe would have liked terribly to have a stick-candy cane. He came a little closer to Santa Claus. He was right in the front of the crowd. And then Santa Claus saw Joe.

Why is it that lots of white people always grin when they see a Negro child? Santa Claus grinned. Everybody else grinned, too, looking at little black Joe—who had no business in the lobby of a white theatre. Then Santa Claus stooped down and slyly picked up one of his lucky number rattles, a great big loud tin-pan rattle like they use in cabarets. And he shook it fiercely right at Joe. That was funny. The white people laughed, kids and all. But little Joe didn't laugh. He was scared. To the shaking of the big rattle, he turned and fled out of the warm lobby of the theatre, out into the street where the snow was and the people. Frightened by laughter, he had begun to cry. He went looking for his mama. In his heart he never thought Santa Claus shook great rattles at children like that—and then laughed.

In the crowd on the street he went the wrong way. He couldn't find the ten-cent store or his mother. There were too many people, all white people, moving like white shadows in the snow, a world of white people.

It seemed to Joe an awfully long time till he suddenly saw Arcie, dark and worried-looking, cut across the side-walk through the passing crowd and grab him. Although her arms were full of packages, she still managed with one free hand to shake him until his teeth rattled.

"Why didn't you stand there where I left you?" Arcie demanded loudly. "Tired as I am, I got to run all over the streets in the night lookin' for you. I'm a great mind to wear you out."

When little Joe got his breath back, on the way home, he told his mama he had been in the moving picture show.

"But Santa Claus didn't give me nothin'," Joe said tearfully. "He made a big noise at me and I runned out."

"Serves you right," said Arcie, trudging through the snow. "You had no business in there. I told you to stay where I left you."

"But I seed Santa Claus in there," little Joe said, "so I went in."

"Huh! That wasn't no Santa Claus," Arcie explained. "If it was, he wouldn't a-treated you like that. That's a theatre for white folks—I told you once—and he's just a old white man."

"Oh . . . ," said little Joe.

Santa Claus Is a White Man

∞

JOHN HENRIK CLARKE

John Henrik Clarke

John Henrik Clarke, a sharecropper's son, was born in Alabama in 1915, but grew up in Columbus, Georgia. In 1933, attracted by tales of the literary and cultural developments spawned by the Harlem Renaissance, he traveled to New York to study creative writing at Columbia University. Immersing himself in the creative and political activities that flourished in Harlem, within a short span of years he was publishing his short stories, poems, articles, and book reviews in magazines and newspapers. During the early years of his career, Clarke was the cofounder and fiction editor of the *Harlem Quarterly*, a book review editor of the *Negro History Bulletin*, an associate editor of *Freedomways* magazine, and a contributor and feature writer for several African and African-American newspapers.

At his death in July 1998, Clarke was described as "an academic original." This tribute paid homage to a man who was in essence an American original. Historically, he is among a few people who were able to obtain an academic teaching position at a major institution of higher learning without benefit of formal training. Beginning as a lecturer in 1969, Clarke enjoyed a long and distinguished tenure as a professor of black and Puerto Rican Studies at Hunter College in New York City and established the Black Studies program there. A largely self-educated man, Clarke was an eighth-grade dropout who eventually took courses at New York University and Columbia. He earned his doctorate in 1993. Through his teachings, writings, and speeches, he distinguished himself as one of the leading black intellectuals of his time. Known as a scholar of African history, he spurred the movement to develop Black Studies and became one of Harlem's leading intellectuals.

Clarke wrote six books, edited and contributed to seventeen others, composed more than fifty short stories, published articles and pamphlets, and helped to found or edit several important black periodicals. His edited collections included *American Negro Short Stories* (1966), *Malcolm X: The Man and His Times* (1969), *Harlem U.S.A.* (1971), and *Marcus Garvey and the Vision of Africa* (1973).

In December 1938, Elmer H. Carter, the editor of *Opportunity*, wrote in an editorial, "The same stars that guided the wise men now looks down upon the onward sweep of racial prejudice, religious bigotry and intolerance; . . . The bells ring out — 'Peace on Earth, Good Will to Men.' But fear peers from the haunted faces of the Jews in Germany — and Justice tosses a Negro boy into the hands of a lynch mob in Mississippi." This incident inspired Clarke to write his first short story, "Santa Claus Is a White Man," published by *Opportunity* in December 1939.

This story explores the multidimensionality of Southern racism and explodes the myth about the goodness of Santa Claus. As a cultural icon, Santa Claus enjoyed a mythical status, which defined him as a benevolent figure, whose legendary love and generosity transcended the boundaries of race, religion, class, and ethnicity. However, the Southern white Santa Claus could, in fact, be the opposite of this, and could pose a threat to a black person's very existence.

Focusing on the central character Randolph Johnson, "the happiest little colored boy in all Louisiana," Clarke demonstrates the need for black parents to educate their children about the real identity of Santa Claus, and uses social realism to tell the story of how little value a black life had during the era of lynching in the South.

Santa Claus Is a White Man

ھ

When he left the large house where his mother was a servant, he was happy. She had embraced him lovingly and had given him—for the first time in his life!—a quarter. "Now you go do your Chris'mus shopping," she had said. "Get somethin' for Daddy and something for Baby and something for Aunt Lil. And something for Mummy too, if it's any money left."

He had already decided how he would divide his fortune. A nickel for something for Daddy, another nickel for Baby, another for Aunt Lil. And ten whole cents for Mummy's present. Something beautiful and gorgeous, like a string of pearls, out of the ten-cent store.

His stubby legs moved fast as he headed toward the business district. Although it was mid-December, the warm southern sun brought perspiration flooding to his little, dark skinned face. He was so happy . . . exceedingly happy! Effortlessly he moved along, feeling light and free, as if the wind was going to sweep him up to the heavens, up where everybody could see him—Randolph Johnson, the happiest little colored boy in all Louisiana!

When he reached the outskirts of the business district, where the bulk of the city's poor-whites lived, he slowed his pace. He felt instinctively that if he ran, one of them would accuse him of having stolen something; and if he moved too slow, he might be charged with looking for something to steal. He walked along with quick, cautious strides, glancing about fearfully now and then. Temporarily the happiness which the prospect of going Christmas shopping had brought him was subdued.

He passed a bedraggled Santa Claus, waving a tinny bell beside a cardboard chimney. He did not hesitate even when the tall fat man smiled at him through whiskers that were obviously cotton. He had seen the one real Santa weeks ago, in a big department store downtown, and had asked for all the things he wanted. This forlorn figure was merely one of Santa's helpers, and he had no time to waste on him just at the moment.

Further down the street he could see a gang of white boys, urchins of the street, clustered about an outdoor fruit stand. They were stealing apples, he was sure. He saw the white-aproned proprietor rush out; saw them disperse in all directions like a startled flock of birds, then gather together again only a few hundred feet ahead of him.

Apprehension surged through his body as the eyes of the gang leader fell upon him. Fear gripped his heart, and his brisk pace slowed to a cautious walk. He decided to cross the street to avoid the possibility of an encounter with this group of dirty ragged white boys.

As he stepped from the curb the voice of the gang leader barked a sharp command. "Hey you, come here!"

The strange, uncomfortable fear within him grew. His eyes widened and every muscle in his body trembled with sudden uneasiness. He started to run, but before he could do so a wall of human flesh had been pushed around him. He was forced back onto the sidewalk, and each time he tried to slip through the crowd of laughing white boys he was shoved back abruptly by the red-headed youngster who led the others.

He gazed dumbfoundedly over the milling throng which was surrounding him, and was surprised to see that older persons, passersby, had joined to watch the fun. He looked back up the street, hopefully, toward the bell-ringing Santa Claus, and was surprised to find him calmly looking on from a safe distance, apparently enjoying the excitement.

He could see now that there was no chance to escape the gang until they let him go, so he just stood struggling desperately to steady his trembling form. His lips twitched nervously and the perspiration on his round black face reflected a dull glow. He could not think; his mind was heavy with confusion.

The red-headed boy was evidently the leader. He possessed a robustness that set him off from the others. They stared impatiently at him, waiting for his next move. He shifted his position awkwardly and spoke with all the scorn that he could muster:

"Whereya goin', nigger? An' don't you know we don't allow niggers in this neighborhood?"

His tone wasn't as harsh as he had meant it to be. It sounded a bit like poor play-acting.

"I'm jes' goin' to the ten-cent store," the little black boy said meekly. "Do my Chris'mus shopping."

He scanned the crowd hurriedly, hoping there might be a chance of escape. But he was completely engulfed. The wall of people about him was rapidly thickening; restless, curious people, laughing at him because he was frightened. Laughing and sneering at a little colored boy who had done nothing wrong, and harmed no one.

He began to cry. "Please, lemme go. I ain't done nothin'."

One of the boys said, "Aw, let 'im go." His suggestion was abruptly laughed down. The red-headed boy held up his hand. "Wait a minute, fellers," he said. "This nigger's goin' shoppin', he must have money, huh? Maybe we oughta see how much he's got."

The little black boy pushed his hand deeper into his pocket and clutched his quarter frantically. He looked about the outskirts of the crowd for a sympathetic adult face. He saw only the fat, sloppy-looking white man in the bedraggled Santa Claus suit that he had passed a moment earlier. This strange, cotton-bearded apparition was shoving his way now through the cluster of people, shifting his huge body along in gawky, poorly timed strides like a person cursed with a subnormal mentality.

When he reached the center of the circle within which the frightened boy was trapped, he waved the red-haired youth aside and, yanking off his flowing whiskers, took command of the situation.

"What's yo' name, niggah?" he demanded.

The colored boy swallowed hard. He was more stunned than frightened; never in his life had he imagined Santa—or even one of Santa's helpers—in a role like this.

"My name's Randolph," he got out finally.

A smile wrinkled the leathery face of the man in the tattered red suit.

"Randolph," he exclaimed, and there was a note of mockery in his tone. "Dat's no name fer er niggah! No niggah's got no business wit er nice name like dat!" Then, bringing his broad hand down forcefully on the boy's shoulder, he added, "Heah after yo' name's Jem!"

His words boomed over the crowd in a loud, brusque tone, defying all other sound. A series of submerged giggles sprang up among the boys as they crowded closer to get a better glimpse of the unmasked Santa Claus and the little colored boy.

The latter seemed to have been decreasing in size under the heavy intensity of their gaze. Tears mingled with the perspiration flooding his round black face. Numbness gripped his body.

"Kin I go on now?" he pleaded. His pitifully weak tone was barely audible. "My momma told me to go straight to the ten-cent store. I ain't been botherin' nobody."

"If you don't stop dat damn cryin', we'll send you t'see Saint Peter." The fat white man spoke with anger and disgust. The cords in his neck quivered and new color came to his rough face, lessening its haggardness. He paused as if reconsidering what he had just said, then added: "Second thought, don't think we will ... Don't think Saint Peter would have anything t' do with a nigger."

The boys laughed long and heartily. When their laughter diminished, the red-coated man shifted his gawky figure closer to the little Negro and scanned the crowd, impatient and undecided.

"Let's lynch 'im," one of the youths cried.

"Yeah, let's lynch 'im!" another shouted, much louder and with more enthusiasm.

As if these words had some magic attached to them, they swept through the crowd. Laughter, sneers, and queer, indistinguishable mutterings mingled together.

Anguish was written on the boy's dark face.

Desperately he looked about for a sympathetic countenance.

The words, "Let's lynch him," were a song now, and the song was floating through the December air, mingling with the sounds of tangled traffic.

"I'll get a rope!" the red-haired boy exclaimed. Wedging his way through the crowd, he shouted gleefully, "Just wait'll I get back!"

Gradually an ominous hush fell over the crowd. They stared questioningly, first at the frightened boy, then at the fat man dressed like Santa Claus who towered over him.

"What's that you got in yo' pocket?" the fat man demanded suddenly.

Frightened, the boy quickly withdrew his hands from his pockets and put them behind his back. The white man seized the right one and forced it open. On seeing its contents, his eyes glittered with delight.

"Ah, a quarter!" he exclaimed. "Now tell me, niggah, where in th' hell did you steal this?"

"Didn't steal hit," the boy tried to explain. "My momma gived it to me."

"Momma gived it to you, heh?" The erstwhile Santa Claus snorted. He took the quarter and put it in a pocket of his red suit. "Niggahs ain't got no business wit' money whilst white folks is starving," he said. "I'll jes keep this quarter for myself."

Worry spread deep lines across the black boy's forehead. His lips parted, letting out a short, muted sob. The crowd around him seemed to blur.

As far as his eyes could see, there were only white people all about him. One and all they sided with the curiously out-of-place Santa Claus. Ill-nourished children, their dirty, freckled faces lighted up in laughter. Men clad in dirty overalls, showing their tobacco-stained teeth. Women whose rutted faces had never known cosmetics, moving their bodies restlessly in their soiled housedresses. . . .

Here suddenly the red-coated figure held up his hand for silence. He looked down at the little black boy and a new expression was on his face. It was not pity; it was more akin to a deep irksomeness. When the crowd quieted slightly, he spoke.

"Folks," he began hesitantly, "ah think this niggah's too lil'l t' lynch. Besides, it's Christmas time . . ."

"What's that got to do with it?" someone yelled.

"Well," the fat man answered slowly, "it jus' ain't late 'nuf in the season. 'Taint got cold yet round these parts. In this weather a lynched niggah would make the whole neighborhood smell bad."

A series of disappointed grunts belched up from the crowd. Some laughed; others stared protestingly at the red-coated white man. They were hardly pleased with his decision.

However, when the red-haired boy returned with a length of rope, the "let's lynch 'im" song had died down. He handed the rope to the white man, who took it and turned it over slowly in his gnarled hands.

"Sorry, sonny," he said. His tone was dry, with a slight tremor. He was not firmly convinced that the decision he had reached was the best one. "We 'sided not to lynch him; he's too lil'l and it's too warm yet. And besides, what's one lil'l niggah who ain't ripe enough to be lynched? Let's let 'im live awhile . . . maybe we'll get 'im later."

The boy frowned angrily. "Aw, you guys!" he groaned. "T' think of all th' trouble I went to gettin' that rope . . ."

In a swift, frenzied gesture his hand was raised to strike the little black boy, who curled up, more terrified than ever. But the bedraggled Santa stepped between them.

"Wait a minute, sonny," he said. "Look a here." He put his hand in the pocket of his suit and brought forth the quarter, which he handed to the red-haired boy.

A smile came to the white youth's face and flourished into jubilant laughter. He turned the quarter from one side to the other in the palm of his hand, marveling at it. Then he held it up so the crowd could see it, and shouted gleefully, "Sure there's a Santa Claus!"

The crowd laughed heartily.

Still engulfed by the huge throng, still bewildered beyond words, the crestfallen little colored boy stood whimpering. They had taken his fortune from him and there was nothing he could do about it. He didn't know what to think about Santa Claus now. About anything, in fact.

He saw that the crowd was falling back, that in a moment there would be a path through which he could run. He waited until it opened, then sped through it as fast as his stubby legs could carry him. With every step a feeling of thankfulness swelled within him.

The red-haired boy who had started the spectacle threw a rock after him. It fell short. The other boys shouted jovially, "Run, nigger, run!" The erstwhile Santa Claus began to readjust his mask.

The mingled chorus of jeers and laughter was behind the little colored boy, pushing him on like a great invisible force. Most of the crowd stood on the side walk watching him until his form became vague and finally disappeared around a corner . . .

After a while he felt his legs weakening. He slowed down to a brisk walk, and soon found himself on the street that pointed toward his home.

Crestfallen, he looked down at his empty hands and thought of the shiny quarter that his mother had given him. He closed his right hand tightly, trying to pretend that it was still there. But that only hurt the more.

Gradually the fear and worry disappeared from his face. He was now among his neighbors, people that he knew. He felt bold and relieved. People smiled at him, said "Hello." The sun had dried his tears.

He decided he would tell no one, except his mother, of his ordeal. She, perhaps, would understand, and either give him a new quarter or do his shopping for him. But what would she say about that awful figure of a Santa Claus? He decided not to ask her. There were some things no one, not even mothers, could explain.

❧ SOURCES ❧

Margaret Black
   "The Woman: A Christmas Story," *Baltimore Afro-American,* December 25, 1915.

J. B. Moore Bristor
   "Found After Thirty-Five Years — Lucy Marshall's Letter — A True Story for Christmas," *Christian Recorder,* December 27, 1883.

Frederick W. Burch
   "For Love of Him: A Christmas Story," *Indianapolis Freeman,* December 21, 1889.

John Henrik Clarke
   "Santa Claus Is a White Man," *Opportunity,* December 1939. Reprinted in Langston Hughes, ed., *The Best Short Stories by Black Writers: The Classic Anthology from 1899 to 1967.* New York: Little Brown and Company, 1967.

Augustus Michael Hodges
   "The Blue and the Gray," *Indianapolis Freeman,* December 29, 1900.
   "Three Christmas Eves," *Indianapolis Freeman,* December 26, 1903.

Pauline Elizabeth Hopkins
   "General Washington: A Christmas Story," *Colored American Magazine,* December 1900.
   [as Sarah A. Allen]
   "The Test of Manhood: A Christmas Story," *Colored American Magazine,* December 1902.

J. B. Howard
   "Thou Shalt Be," *Indianapolis Freeman,* March 12, 1903.

Langston Hughes
   "One Christmas Eve," *Opportunity*, December 1933. Reprinted in Langston Hughes, *The Ways of White Folks*. New York: Alfred A. Knopf, Inc., 1934.

Mary Jenness
   "A Carol of Color," *Opportunity*, December 1927.

Georgia Douglas Johnson
   "Christmas Greetings," *Opportunity*, December 1923.

Mildred E. Lambert
   "A Christmas Sketch," *Christian Recorder*, December 28, 1882.

Mary E. Lee
   "Mollie's Best Christmas Gift," *Christian Recorder*, December 31, 1885.

Lelia Plummer
   "The Autobiography of a Dollar Bill," *Colored American Magazine*, December 1904.

Eva S. Purdy
   "How I Won My Husband: A Christmas Story," *Baltimore Afro-American*, December 24, 1910.

Louis Lorenzo Redding
   "A Christmas Journey," *Opportunity*, December 1925.

Bruce L. Reynolds
   "It Came to Pass: A Christmas Story," *Chicago Defender*, December 23, 1939.

Carrie Jane Thomas
   "A Christmas Story," *Christian Recorder*, December 24, 1885.

Katherine Davis Tillman
   "Fannie May's Christmas," *Christian Recorder*, December 29, 1921.